Bottom of the Well

Bottom of the Well

Patrick Carpenter

"Fear is pain arising from the anticipation of evil."

~ Aristotle

5 points of emotional interest ...

1: Anxiety

2: Test of Will

3: Fight or Flight

4: True Test

5: Climax

Be aware ... outcomes may pale to perceptions

Bottom of the Well

Copyright © 2022 Patrick Carpenter

All rights reserved. No part of this book may be used or reproduced in any manner without the prior written permission of the copyright owner, except for the use of brief quotations in which the copyright owner is credited or for the purpose of a book review.

1st edition paperback, hardcover, and Ebook published August 2022 by Epic Arts Publications.

Ebook ISBN: 978-1-7362255-4-7
Paperback: ISBN: 978-1-7362255-2-3
Hardcover ISBN: 978-1-7362255-3-0

For permissions or inquiries about Bottom of the Well, please visit **epicartspc.com.**

*Be advised: Bottom of the Well contains some scenes involving cursing, violence, gore, and consensual sex.

Foreword

To those brave enough to indulge in the twistedness of my mind, thank you for taking the journey. This is my second completed novel, and my first attempt at the horror genre. I've thoroughly enjoyed writing this piece as it's a fast-paced, suspenseful, and intense! A lovely side venture from my Dark Ocean series, of which plenty more will come. I hope you enjoy the read!

Check out my first novel, Dark Ocean, on Amazon, and visit my website for sample chapters: epicartspc.com

Bottom of the Well

Bottom of the Well

Patrick Carpenter

Bottom of the Well

1

I found myself surrounded by the dread of nightmares. My senses were assaulted by fear of the unknown; the damp pitch-black air; the smell of mildew; the tense, anticipatory silence.

"Hello? Hello!" I cried. "Hello! Is anyone there? Where am I?" My voice seemed instantly swallowed by the blackness.

I became aware of my wrists, bound by steel cuffs led by thick chains laid across the dirt. My heart was racing now, and I decided to follow my chains to the source, where I felt a massive iron block wedged deep into the ground beneath the thick ring where the last links of my chains were connected. *Why am I chained up?* Panic started setting in. Searching the area surrounding the block, I felt bumpy, coarse stone walls, a dirt floor, and nothing else.

What is this place? Who brought me here?

I was abducted; that's probably why my head hurt. Someone hit me over the head, knocked me out, and dragged me into this dungeon.

"Hello! Help me! Is anyone there? Help me!" I knew it was pointless, what I was doing. No one could hear me except whatever twisted individual had brought me here. Tears started forming, streaking down my cheeks as I shuffled up and down the wall, searching for any variation in texture, any sliver of hope that there was a door or a weak spot in the wall, or anything but whatever awaited me here.

"Please!" I tried one more time before resorting to something even more pointless: bunching up the chains around my fist, I leaned back and tugged with all my might. I grunted and groaned as I exerted as much of myself as I could, pulling up, down, left, and right, then over my shoulder with all my weight. Frustrated, I shook the chains, and as the jangling of the metal echoed deep into the darkness, I screamed, "Fuck! What the hell is this?"

My intensity tapered off over several minutes, at least, I assumed it was several minutes, because it was impossible to tell time in my state. Eventually, I retreated into the corner of the room and sat against the wall, wrapping my arms around my knees and pressing them to my chest. I cried quietly as all the diabolical scenarios began to eat my brain. I was in real trouble. This was really elaborate, not the doing of just any kidnapper. He made some secret underground dungeon, captured me, chained me up here ... and however he got me, I couldn't remember at all. *He is going to rape me, torture me, and kill me. How long will he keep me alive before he kills me? Will anyone be able to find me here? Oh God, how bad will it hurt?*

If I kept thinking about it, my head was going to explode. I had to stay positive! If he hadn't already killed me, it meant he wanted something from me, which meant I had a chance to live. I just had to figure out what he wanted or simply stay alive long enough for someone to figure out I was missing and come find me. How likely was that? The last place I was before here was ... my dad's house? My sister Ginny and I were there. No, that was earlier in the night. I went to class that morning, and then I stopped at my dad's to get changed ... that's right. We went to a party after that. Someone must have drugged me there.

I hope Ginny is not here somewhere.

When I reached the other end of my rainbow of emotions, I was sitting in the dirt, my face wet and sticky from the tears, and everything went still. I was held captive by the chains, but it was the darkness to which I felt most bound. The silence was palpable. I don't know how to describe it exactly, but I knew something was out there. Maybe it was the thickness of the air, or perhaps the hollowness of the quiet. I don't even know what that means, but it's what I felt, like if a breeze went through the corridor at that moment, I'd hear a whistle in the wall. *Wait, that's it!*

With renewed vigor, I threw myself against the wall, running my fingers along the spaces between the rocks, much harder and more deliberately now than before. The masonry felt old and withered. Where was this place anyway? A basement? It was impossible to tell, but it definitely seemed manmade. I scrambled along the wall, feeling through every crack, looking for any sign of difference, until I met the corner of the room where I had awoken, then I started along the back wall too. There were much fewer rocks on this one. Honestly, I had no idea what I was looking for, but I had this gut feeling.

I heard a shuffling noise. Feet dragging along the dirt. It seemed far away, yet not far enough.

Whatever it was, it was coming toward me.

Oh God!

I wanted to scream, but instead I listened, hoping maybe I'd heard wrong.

Another shuffle.

Panic returned as I spun back toward the dark abyss in front of my chain block, my eyes darting with wild instinct, searching for whoever, or whatever, I sensed out there.

My attention was soon diverted as I heard a voice calling faintly, "Hello? Is anyone there? Hello!" It sounded like a male voice, far away and muffled.

Elated to hear someone else's voice, I yelled back, "Hello! Hello? Where are you? Can you hear me?"

"I hear you! Can you see anything?"

I thought I could hear tears in his voice. The

kidnapper must have brought him there as well. All at once, I was terrified, sympathetic, and surprisingly, slightly reassured. At least I wasn't alone.

"No, it's pitch black."

"Where are we?"

"I don't know, I just woke up here."

As I listened to his voice, I realized the reason it was muffled was because it was coming from the other side of the wall. Just as I suspected, the walls were not as thick as they appeared.

He yelled again, "What's your name?"

"Lani. Lani Talbot, and yours?"

"Lani?!" The inflection in his voice changed as he heard my name, as if he recognized me.

"Yes? What's your name?"

"Lani, it's me, Jake. Jake Thompson. Are you ok? Where are you; I can't see you? What the hell is going on?"

Jake Thompson? I did know him! We went to school together, but why ... why were we here?

I took a moment to process it, then responded, "I'm ok. Listen, Jake, I'm on the other side of the wall. It's not too thick. I think there is a hole somewhere. That's why we can hear each other."

"Is anyone else in here?"

"I don't know. Jake, help me find the hole. I know it's here somewhere."

While we were talking, I was feeling along the wall again, following the sound of Jake's voice. No sign of a weakness yet, and I was getting toward the end of my chain's reach. I got to thinking more about Jake. He had been at that party too. Whoever did this to us must have been there, but how did he drug both of us without anyone noticing? Was anyone else from the party here? *God, please don't let Ginny be here.*

"It's all solid, I got nothing," Jake said.

"Keep looking."

I reached above my head to where it seemed like a rock was jutting out further from the wall than the rest, and as I did, I felt the chain stiffen and stop my hand just before the rock. I heard the shuffling sound again.

"Jake?" I prayed it was him as I felt my heartbeat speed up. He didn't answer right away, and my eyes started darting around again. I was suddenly aware, much more acutely than when I had initially woken in this place, of the gravity of the situation I was in. Scenarios started to play out in my head, like what happens if no one can find me, what I might have to do to escape these chains, then ... my heart about fucking stopped.

"Lani? Are you there? I'm chained up, I can't go any further."

I could hear him, but I couldn't speak. I couldn't move. There, at the edge of the darkness before me, was the faintest silhouette. In the darkness, it was impossible to tell how far away it was. Not knowing for sure was the worst part. But I had this gut feeling; someone was on my side of the wall, and I just knew he was there to get me.

2

"Lani? Lani! Are you still there? Come on, don't leave me hanging in here!"

Jake's voice was a distant whisper compared to the deafening sound of my fear. I swear I saw the mysterious outline moving, swaying from side to side, watching me. I couldn't do it. I couldn't look at it anymore. As I slammed my eyes shut, my lip quivered and my body shuddered with dread. My heart thumped into my ears, the blood rushing to my brain so fast my face was burning and my forehead was pulsing. I wanted to answer Jake, but I was frozen in fear.

"Lani?" Jake was still going.

Aside from Jake's hollering, nothing seemed to be happening. I mustered all my courage and opened my eyes. Whatever had been there before seemed to be gone.

I shushed him. "Listen for a minute. Someone is here." I imagined that Jake's heart must have dropped then, just as mine had the moment before. The terrible silence ensued while I searched the blackness. I had to be sure.

Nothing. Not a trace of my stalker.

A long thirty seconds passed before Jake said, "I

don't hear anything."

"Maybe I imagined it," I replied. *No way. Wishful thinking.* He was out there. I just couldn't think of a reason to drag Jake into that hell of mine, not yet. "Well, either way, *someone* brought us here. We have to find a way out, fast, before he comes for us."

"There is nothing here, Lani."

"That's not true, Jake. Look around; what resources do you have on your side?"

"Resources? It's fucking dirt and rocks. Nothing else is in here."

"No, look harder. Even the slightest thing can be useful."

As I corrected Jake, I started telling him what I was doing so he could copy my tactics. I began feeling around my side of the wall again, this time focusing more on the ground and the area around the base of my chain block. I ran my finger along every inch of the big metal ring on top of the block and the links attached to it, searching for weakness. This inspired me to inspect every individual link in my chain. Even one weak one could've been key. Were there any loose rocks on the ground, perhaps one large enough to break one of the links? My hands began dashing around the dirt, then along the base of the chain block. For a second, I thought that maybe I could dig deep enough to pull out the whole block.

The whole time I was thinking of my sister, Ginny.

Anytime we went somewhere potentially dangerous, she would always roll her eyes at me, annoyed as I rattled off lists of emergency precautions. We used to go camping all the time, and that was when I would be the most proactive. What if a bear came, I'd ask her, or what if there was a flash flood while we were in our tents, or what if one of us breaks our ankle while hiking?

Don't get me wrong; camping with my family was one of my favorite things. My dad had this little rubber boat he'd take me fishing on—I'd laugh at him because we had this big fancy truck and all this gear, and yet he'd always insist on the rubber boat. It was more intimate, he'd say. Fishing was about peace. Then there was hiking, and cooking over the fire, and staying up late with Ginny while we lay in our tent, fooling around and playing with our headlamps. Those were some of my favorite memories. I loved the outdoors, for sure, but it could be dangerous. That was my point.

Ginny would always say those things wouldn't happen, but I would keep on going, telling her which types of bears not to run from and how to properly set a broken bone and whatever else I could think of. I was just making certain that we were always prepared in case anything happened. I thought it was better to know and not need the information, than to need the information and not know it. I felt like I could have more fun when I knew we were being safe. As we got older, Ginny started to be more aware of things, like me. I was glad my prepper mentality had some effect on her. I could only hope that mentality would be my lifeline now, in this hell I've found myself in.

I continued to instruct Jake, telling him to look for loose rocks on the wall to use for smashing the chain block, loose pieces of metal or anything to pick the locks on the shackles, and about a half a dozen other semi-natural items that the kidnapper may have felt too harmless to remove from the area. I asked Jake if he still had shoes, and if so, did they have those little metal lace hooks? My thought was, maybe we could file through the masonry if he could rip off those.

After maybe ten minutes of this, Jake said, "This is hopeless, Lani. Whoever did this to us is too smart."

"It's not hopeless, keep looking."

All the true crime podcasts I had ever watched were playing in my head, rapid firing like Tik Tok reels of death and depravity. My friends used to joke with me that I was sadistic, always watching the most fucked-up stories and getting so wrapped up in them. I was laughing then because, well, it *was* a little sadistic. But I learned a lot from watching those, and boy was I glad for that now. Maybe the most important thing I learned was that sometimes the people in these impossible situations got away, and they did it in the most unlikely of ways. I once watched a video where a woman was held captive in a remote part of the Appalachian Mountains. The guy had her in a cage in nothing but underwear in the basement below his log cabin for nine days before she escaped, and the only reason she got out was because of her ingenuity with everyday items. See, this man, he had a habit of picking his teeth. Every time he came down to the basement, he had a toothpick or something hanging out of his mouth. He would chomp on that thing to the point of being irritating. Pick, pick, pick. One day the guy forgot the toothpick, so he reached over to his workstation and grabbed a thin little nail. After he gave her a good beating, he started picking his teeth with the nail. She saw the opportunity and grabbed his leg, and in the subsequent tussle, the nail fell on the floor. When the guy was done fucking her up for this insubordination, he went back upstairs. The clever woman then used the nail to pick the lock and get the hell out.

If she could do that, I could escape from here. I just had to find my skinny little nail.

"Lani!" Jake snapped me back into reality. "I found something!"

I leapt up with excitement.

"Jake? Tell me what you see."

"It's a lighter!" Jake shouted. "I found a lighter!"

Eagerly, I pressed my body against the wall to hear him better. "Does it work?" I heard the familiar flicking sound of the striker against the flint.

Jake's excitement rose. "Yes! It works!" He started laughing about it and I heard him strike the flame again. Instantly, I thought of my dad, sitting in his parlor, lighting up a cigar while he rapped away at his keyboard. I never really knew what he was working on in there. All I knew was he ran a business with my granddad, who still lived in Brazil. My dad moved to The States when he was in his twenties, where he met my mother and moved to Pennsylvania, where we lived now. Whatever he was working on, he never seemed to be done with it. I could practically smell the maple cedar smoke, hear my dad blowing the smoke in between sounds of fingers typing and midcentury jazz filling the background. I had to stop myself from crying. I'd have given anything to be there right now.

"Hold on," I said, swallowing hard and trying to keep myself level. "Don't waste it. We don't know what it is good for yet." Regardless of my warning, I could hear Jake meandering about, periodically flicking the lighter. Trying not to sound curt, I asked, "Can you see anything? Don't waste it if you can't see anything."

"It's too dark. I can't see down the tunnel, but I can see the walls up close. I am looking for the hole."

At this idea I perked up. "Yes! If you find the hole, mark it somehow, so we can get back to it without the light." Although I had no idea what significance it would have if we could accomplish that, I was determined to stay goal oriented. All the women who escaped in those videos were always working on something. Not every idea was good, but the worst idea of all was no idea.

A moment passed and I thought of a way to expand upon the hole. "Jake, we can use our shackles to file through the masonry. I bet it is weaker near the hole." To test my theory, I bent my arm and felt around for the rivet where the chain links connected to my shackles. Then I pressed the curved metal between two of the rocks and began sawing up and down along the grout. Immediately I realized this was a fool's errand. The sharp, uneven rock surfaces on either side of the grout tore at my forearm if I even gave the slightest effort at it. I moved a few inches down, searching for flatter rocks. It didn't make much of a difference. And what the hell was I even going to do once I got through the wall? I was still chained to a block.

"We can't get through this," Jake said as the sound of his chains rattling and metal grating on stone fell off.

Furious at the failure, I stood up and leaned all my weight toward the wall, found myself a good spot, and went to town like a hunter with a hacksaw. My skin was rubbed raw and covered with tiny cuts from doing this, but my adrenaline was masking most of it. Finally, I screamed out of frustration and thrust my hands through the air, the rattling sound of my chains echoing down the dark hallway. I fell to my knees, facing the corner where I had woken. I let myself cry for a moment. I think it was right then, as I felt the burning pain traveling up and down my arm and felt a slight bit of blood trickle from one of the cuts, and I felt the truth of the darkness around me, the hopeless, pervasive blackness, that I knew I was in real trouble. *I might never see Ginny again. Or my father, or my friends, or ... hell, I might never even see the sun again.*

If I didn't figure things out, I was going to die in this place.

I fell onto my hands and let my head hang over the dirt. My eyes were still moist, but I fought the urge to keep crying. I was starting to let it get to me, all of this, and if I did that I was going to give up. I had to stay positive.

Then I heard it again. That same shuffling sound, coming from what seemed like pretty far down the dark hallway behind me.

"Jake?"

More shuffling, now a little closer.

"Jake, do you hear that?"

"Hear what?"

"Shhh!" I commanded. Dead silence for a moment, the kind you could blow an eardrum with. *Wait a minute.* Something was coming into view. Wait ... no it wasn't. The shuffling noise quickened, then petered out. I thought I heard rattling in the distance, but that could have been

Jake's chains. Hell, even my own. I was so fixated with fear that I couldn't decide.

"I hear it," Jake said.

Paralysis washed over me momentarily with Jake's validation. If he heard it too, it had to be real. I started taking careful, quiet steps back toward the corner, my heart slamming out of my chest. There was no way to explain it, and I couldn't see anything there, but I knew there was something in the dark, just beyond the cusp of reality.

Two more sounds echoed in the darkness before all went silent again, and it went silent for a long time. So long, actually, that Jake and I had run out of things to distract ourselves talking about. The presence I had sensed seemed to be gone, but I was certain I hadn't imagined it. Something had been there.

As time slowly trickled on, I sat there in my corner, messing with my chain block, trying to figure out a way to beat it. I kept thinking; even if I got through part of that wall somehow, or found some other way out of that room, it wouldn't matter if I couldn't get out of the chains. After a while, I shifted my focus from the block to the shackles on my wrists. Maybe I could squeeze through them. I thought *maybe* it was possible, if I broke my wrist, but I wasn't sure, and I wasn't breaking my wrist for nothing. Plus, I'd have to break both. No way that would work. Eventually I grew tired and sat myself against the wall.

There was another long silence after I let my chains fall into the dirt beside me. Jake must have been asleep; I hadn't heard him moving in a little while. As I laid my head against the stone and closed my eyes, I began to reminisce about the night before. Jake and I had been discussing it while I was working on the block—both of us had some pretty scattered memories of it. It was weird. Whatever drug we were given must have impacted our ability to remember. Or maybe we were just really drunk, I don't know. But either way, there wasn't very much crossover between our experiences. From what we did remember, we both seemed to agree that whatever had happened to us must have happened either at the party or right after.

That thought prompted me to feel up and down my body. I was wearing a Henley and a pair of jeans. I had on a bra underneath, no underwear, and no shoes. My hair was down. Was there some correlation to where I was the previous night? I racked my brain, but I couldn't remember putting on jeans. I had a party dress ... and I'd been wearing hoops. I felt my ears, but the hoops were gone. Only my two cartilage studs remained. What the hell? I was starting to get anxious, and I decided I needed to slow down, think about things one at a time.

I considered for a moment the first thing I could recall about the previous day, besides being at school, and replayed it in my mind. It was right around six p.m. when

Bottom of the Well

Ginny and I were at my dad's house, finishing up getting ready to go out, the first time I can remember something weird happening ...

3

"Oh. My. God. YES! You should definitely wear that one!" Ginny had exclaimed as I emerged from the bathroom in a new black party dress I had bought the day before. A slim, flirty thing with plenty of legs and a perfect amount of V-shaped cleavage pulled together by a thin strip of fabric and a dainty gold ring. No straps, all shoulders. They were one of my best features, so naturally I had to buy that dress. Under it, I had my sexy black push up, obviously strapless, and a matching pair of lacey underwear. I tossed a two-piece swimsuit into my purse, just in case. I didn't know how I felt about swimming, but it was better to be prepared, right? I mean, there had to be a pool at a rich guy's house.

"Pretty sexy, right?"

"Um, girl, you're gonna slay. Save some guys for me at least."

"I'll try," I jested. In reality, Ginny was usually the center of attention. Even in my new dress, I wouldn't keep up with her swarm of admirers. It had been that way ever since eighth grade. Ginny just had this aura about her. Guys just instantly loved her. Plus (and I would never say this to Ginny) she had a certain experience level that guys tended to enjoy as well. I was never quite as driven in that way. Except that night. Maybe it was the stress from school, or the fact that it was my first time going out in a while, but whatever it was, I just really felt like getting into trouble. Specifically, there was one guy I thought might be at that party that I wouldn't mind sliding on top of. What a thing that would be, I thought, if I ran into Sami Hyoung, that hot lacrosse player from my college algebra class. A small fire ignited inside me as I craved the thought of him inside of me, my long brunette hair cascading over his face as I leaned over him and slid my hands across his chest. I'd let him do so many things to me.

My fantasy broke apart as Ginny turned on her Spotify app and some poppy R&B song began making my ears bleed.

"Is Cadence coming?" Ginny asked through the side of her mouth as she bent over and inspected her eyelashes up close in the mirror. Cadence was our mutual friend we had known since grade school, but lately she'd been rather distant. All of us had been feeling the pressure from midterms, but it seemed like maybe something more was going on with Cadence. In fact, Ginny and I hadn't seen or heard from her in a couple of days. She wasn't even answering our texts. That's why we invited her—this normally wouldn't be her scene, but Ginny and I thought she could use a night out to clear her mind.

I approached the mirror and put my earrings into my earlobes, a pair of silver hoops with little dangly bits that looked super cute with my dress and heels to match. Not huge hoops, I hated those, but just reasonably sized ones.

Ginny was beside me, bopping about. "You have such shitty taste in music," I said. "And I don't know about Cadence. I texted her."

"Oh, you'd rather listen to emo shit? 'Oh, look at me, I have emotions and I feel lots of stuff and I want you to be sad with me.' Come on, that's not party music!"

"Well, it's not emo music," I corrected. Though, some of it was borderline. It's a fine line between good alternative and grunge.

"Yeah, it's emo music. It's ok. You can be sad, just not tonight." Another giddy, upbeat song came on and Ginny got excited again and started dancing at me. "Tonight, we are partying!"

I took a step aside and grimaced a bit, as I was trying to do mascara and she was distracting me and getting obnoxiously close. "You should text her again," I said, hoping that would get her away. "She isn't texting me back. I know you two are closer."

"Yeah, in a minute." Ginny retreated into the bathroom, and I heard water running and more Spotify echoing off the bathroom walls. Text notifications started blowing up my phone. Call it fate or whatever, the second

I put my mascara away and glanced down at my phone, the screen lit up and Sami's name flashed across the top.

"Heard you might come out tonight?" his text read, with a little tongue-hanging-out emoji after it.

"Maybe," I responded, curious whether he would chase.

I was slipping into my heels when Ginny came out of the bathroom. "You ready to go?"

"Yeah, just a second." One last touch: my most playful ruby-red lipstick.

"Damn, girl …"

"Ok, let's go!" I said with plenty of pep as I grabbed my phone and purse and made for the door.

My phone lit up as we went downstairs. Sami again. "Well, fingers crossed I run into you later :P"

"Hmmm, who is that?" Ginny teased.

I shrugged it off and said, "No one." It was a little odd, this thing with Sami. He was such fire, and at the same time, he was kind of awkward; I was almost embarrassed to say I had a crush on him. I don't know why. Maybe I just wasn't quite old enough to appreciate nerds. I'm sure that's what my dad would say, in his corny dad way.

"Whatever. Come on, you are up to something."

"You're one to talk." Ginny was always up to something, ever since freshman year in high school. It was frustrating, because our parents always thought I was the one who was going to get knocked up for some reason, but I didn't even lose my virginity until I was seventeen. Ginny started having sex in eighth grade, yet that didn't seem to matter. What my parents didn't realize was Ginny's innocent act was just that: a performance. Her charm worked on others too. I don't know why, but I was labeled promiscuous, mean, slutty, or whatever quite frequently. One of my friends said once it was because I wore a lot of makeup and dressed "all fashionista and stuff." That, and apparently I had a resting bitch face. Come to think of it, that was another reason why guys tended to go for Ginny instead of me. They thought I was less approachable.

"You aren't fooling me. I've seen you talking to Jake."

"Jake who?"

We were out the front door now and walking down the stone path from the front door to Ginny's Mini Cooper. The moon was hidden behind a cluster of clouds and the street was eerily dark between its few lamp posts.

"Jake Thompson, you know, that guy from Atlanta? Well, whatever. Anyway ..."

Ginny kept right on, as she often did, and while she was talking a mile a minute, I was carefully checking our surroundings. It was awfully dark out. For the most part, we lived in a safe neighborhood, but I was always careful.

My eyes went up and down both sides of the street to our left, then over the top of the car toward the neighbor's house across the street. Nothing but the patterned spray of water and a continuous clicking sound from their lawn sprinklers. Ginny went around to the driver's side of the car while I waited with my hand on the passenger's side handle. That's about when my eyes scanned to my right, catching sight of something odd. A middle-aged man, probably about my dad's age, leaning against the brick wall that surrounded the property next to ours. He was on the outside of the barrier, facing toward Ginny and I with his hands in his pockets. He wasn't out there smoking or anything, and he wasn't one of the people who lived there. Was he waiting for someone? A taxi, maybe? It didn't seem like he was visiting. Plus, I knew the neighbors, and they were pretty private people. They rarely had guests, and if they did, it wasn't someone weird like this guy.

"Lani?" Ginny said.

"What?" I acknowledged her but kept my eyes on the strange man.

Ginny had opened her car door, then she seemed to notice the man as well. Once we were both looking at him, the man took one hand out of his pocket and gave us a weird two-finger salute, cracking a cocky smile, though I could barely see it beneath the shadow cast by his big, flappy fisherman's hat.

"Do I know you?" I demanded.

"Lani—" Ginny started.

"Prolly not," the man said.

"What are you doing? Are you waiting for someone?" I asked.

"Just in the neighborhood."

Ginny and I shot each other nervous glances and looked back at the man. He hadn't moved or made any indication that he planned on leaving that spot. Was that all he was going to say? I'd be damned. I pressed him, motioning toward the house behind the wall he was leaning on. "Were you visiting the Marinos?"

"Just passing through."

"You don't look like you are passing anywhere," Ginny said. When the man remained silent, she added, "I am going to call the cops."

"Nice lipstick," he replied, as if Ginny hadn't threatened him.

"What?"

"I can see it from here, bright, beaming ... red."

I realized he was talking about me and scowled. "Ok, you creepy asshole, we are calling the cops."

Ginny was already dialing. The guy was mumbling to himself, and I reached into my purse for my pepper spray and kept my eyes carefully fixed on his practically drooling lips. "Red ... bright, sexy red," he kept saying, his eyes agape like a kid in a candy shop.

"Hello? Yes, this is Ginny Talbot, yeah, there is a creepy guy outside my neighbor's house. Yeah, he was here when my sister and I left, and he is just standing there staring at us. It's sixteen Green Grove Circle."

"Big, red lips ... mmmm ... pretty red ruby."

"No, we need someone right now. This guy keeps mumbling about my sister's lips. Sixteen Green Grove Circle."

At the same time Ginny was talking, my nerves went into overdrive. "Shut the fuck up, creep!" I screamed, both in anger and fear of his beady little eyes.

"Ok, yes, thank you, we will." Ginny wrapped up the conversation and hung up. "You hear that, asshole? The cops are coming, and they are going to arrest your creepy ass!"

He mumbled a second more, then, randomly, his normal voice came back. "That's ok. I was just passing through."

Before either me or Ginny could process it, the man darted around the corner of the brick wall and down the property line between the Marino's and my dad's house.

"Hey!" I screamed after the man. I'm not sure what I wanted from him, but it felt like the right reaction.

To add to it, I was about to run after him, but Ginny said, "Lani! Are you nuts?" Instantly, I realized she was right. That was what he wanted, for me to chase him down a dark path into the wooded area behind the houses and away from where the cops were about to be.

"God." I let out a huge breath. "Who the hell does that?"

"I don't know. But I want to get the hell out of here. I'm calling back to let the police know he ran into the woods."

"Good idea."

Ginny and I got into the car, keeping a close eye on our periphery as we did. I imagined that any second that psycho was going to come running back out of the backyard and smash our windows out, beat us to the ground, drag us to whatever hole he came from. My mind always went to places like that. How could it not, though? I mean, what was he doing there?

It seemed so reckless, thinking back. We'd just driven off and went to a party after this creep had been messing with us. And he was behind the house! Did we go home after the party? Were we drunk? That's how he got us. He waited in the backyard, and now I was in this dungeon. Ginny must have been there somewhere too. But Jake ... how does he fit in? I definitely remembered leaving the party, and Jake wasn't with us. In fact, I only saw him for a little while, playing beer pong with me, Ginny, and Cole Diamante, the guy who owned the house.

My thoughts were cut short when, deep into the blackness, something began stirring. Dirt sifted. A rock fell somewhere, echoing off the walls. It sounded faint, faraway.

"Hello?" I called nervously.

Nothing.

"Is someone there?"

I already knew the answer.

The familiar shuffling noises I'd heard earlier started up again, this time closer, more reckless. By the second, they were getting closer and faster.

"Who's there!" Tears began forming in my eyes. This was it. He was coming for me.

Then, the noises stopped. Everything went quiet again. I held my breath and dug my nails into my palms so hard I drew blood. I couldn't even speak.

The silence was shattered by a loud, terrifying roar. The bellow of a beast, echoing with primal rage off the walls of my prison. My instinct was to scream as well, but my naked fear was so intense that my whole body was frozen, even my throat. I felt like I was freezing cold and burning up all at once.

Now the shuffling came back, but in big, sweeping sounds. Running.

"Lani?" Jake yelled, apparently woken by whatever had roared.

And then it appeared.

4

The shadow towered over me, seven feet tall at least, with a broad bulky frame, and just stared at me.

"Please, oh God, please!" I pleaded, raising my shackled arms over my head. As he stepped forward he slumped something onto the ground beside me, then I heard a clanking sound as he knelt down and set something else on the ground. Surprisingly, a light flicked on. An electric lantern.

I looked up at him, now illuminated by the dim orange light. He was dressed in all black and his head was huge, twice the size it ought to be. And he had horns, big ones. The head of a bull? What the hell was I looking at? My heart was beating so fast and the blood was rushing to my head. I nearly fainted as he loomed before me and I cowered back into the corner of the room.

As he looked toward his brown burlap sack, the item he had thrown down beside me, I caught a glimpse of a ring of keys on his waist, and beside it was a huge knife housed snugly in a leather sheath. Dangling from his right arm was a medieval iron axe, one of those heavy two-sided ones with a long metal hilt. His arm muscles bulged out as he lifted the deadly steel just a few inches and slammed it down into the ground beside me. He began rummaging around in the sack. Kneeling across from where I sat, the man, the bull headed thing removed a piece of dark brown fabric from the sack and rolled it out like a carpet between us. On that cloth, he emptied the other contents of the sack one by one, placing them precisely side by side.

All that time, Jake was calling to me, his chains rattling wildly. He knew something was happening, but he didn't know the half of it. Every item on the cloth in front of me was something I might need: a bottle of water, a chunk of bread, a crude dark brown blanket, a book of matches, and a pair of shoes. As the bull-man placed the last item on the fabric, he slouched back and waited, staring intently at me while I considered the spread. The man's hand moved in a slow, calculated manner up and down the hilt of the axe, while the sharp, life-ending curve of steel at the killing end remained partially buried in the dirt beside the cloth table. The black spheres that were his eyes suggested nothing as he sat and waited.

Desperately, I pleaded, "What do you want? Please, let me go!" I knew it was pointless, but I'd be cheating myself if I didn't at least try.

"Lani? What is going on? Is there someone there?" Jake called out. "Whoever you are, if you hurt Lani, I'll kill you!"

The man offered no response. With his free hand, he dove back into the sack, which lay in a floppy heap on the dirt. As he burrowed around the dirty lump of canvas, I pulled my legs up to my chest and clutched them tight, retreating into my corner as far away from him as I could. He produced what looked like a piece of folded parchment paper and held it up in front of him. He slowly lowered the paper and placed it next to the shoes, little crinkling sounds accompanying his actions as he fiddled with it to position it perfectly among the other items.

Now it was back to the stare down.

"Lani? Tell me what is happening!" Jake again.

Through tear-filled eyes, I examined the items in front of me. What kind of sick fuck was this guy? Dressed like a bull, just sitting there, waiting for me to do what? Choose one of those? The way they were arranged, it was clear I wasn't entitled to all the items. I can't explain why, but I just knew it. I was only getting one of those things.

My mind raced with deliberation. Depending on how long I was going to be down there, that bottle of water would be my lifeline. I could probably live without the food. The blanket would be nice. What would the matches be for? Light, I guessed. That would be great, but not essential to being chained up. On the other hand, I didn't plan to remain chained up. So the shoes might be the smartest choice. After all, if I got out, I would have to run, and these bare feet wouldn't cut it. What if I got out of there and it was the middle of nowhere? Some forest full of twigs and thorns and other stuff that would cut my feet? Also, when I got to thinking of escaping, I realized I didn't know how deep this tunnel was where the man came from, nor how many others it might connect to. I might need those matches just to find my way out to begin with. Oh God ... what if I chose the wrong item? Would I get another choice if I survived long enough?

My eyes wandered to the piece of parchment paper. On the top was a crudely drawn question mark in drippy black ink. What the hell? What could possibly be written on the inside of that piece of paper? Maybe it was a map! Or some kind of clue about how to escape. *No, he wouldn't just give that to me.* But for the life of me I couldn't think of what else it would be. It didn't matter, I decided. Whatever was on the paper, it wasn't more important than the survival items, not at that time. I made my decision.

Gingerly, I leaned toward the spread and reached for the water. I desperately wanted the shoes, but I could already feel the thirst creeping up my throat. I wouldn't need the shoes if I died on that chain block first.

I was inches from the water when I felt the man's presence shift. His grip tightened on the axe, and I heard him expel a low grunt. His chest puffed and his feet shifted in the dirt.

"I don't know what you want," I sputtered, pulling my hand away from the water. The man relaxed his grip on the axe. I'd never been so scared and so confused. I almost wished he would just split my skull in half and get it over with.

Jake was yelling with fresh bravado, "Hey, leave Lani alone! Come mess with me, you asshole!"

Meanwhile, the man was still kneeling there, staring holes into me.

"I don't understand," I sobbed, wiping snot from my nose and sucking in exasperated breaths.

He extended a hand toward me, opening his palm face-up, and just waited, like he wanted me to give him something.

"Just tell me what you want and I'll give it to you! Please, I have plenty of money, I can give you anything you want." That plea never worked in the movies, and it sure as hell wasn't going to work with that psycho. I just didn't know what else to say.

The man closed his palm and began to load the items back into the sack, one by one. When he was done, he rolled up the cloth mat, stuffed that into the bag as well, and yanked his axe from the ground. Now he was standing, towering over me, and I was balling myself up in the corner again, saying silent prayers. *Please, just walk away ... just walk away, get that huge axe away from me.*

As if reading my mind, the man silently turned and disappeared back into the darkness from which he had come.

5

I may not have remembered being drugged, but I'll tell you what I would never forget: that scream, the primal roar of the Bull Man before he appeared from the darkness. When he came the second time, it was just as terrifying as the first. The moment I heard it, I retreated to my corner and felt my body tensing up, a cold chill overtaking me as I wrapped myself up into a fetal position.

"Lani?" I heard Jake calling again. At first, I couldn't respond. I was paralyzed, like before. Then I realized I couldn't hear the shuffling noises and I didn't sense him coming for me. Confusion swept over me, and I started to crawl on all fours toward the tunnel, searching timidly for his outline.

"Who are you?" Jake demanded. I heard his chains rattling and feet stomping around. Someone grunted deeply. The Bull Man was on Jake's side!

Realizing what was happening, I scrambled up to the wall and yelled, "Jake! Is he over there? What is happening?"

"Who are you?" Jake questioned the Bull Man. "What are you doing?" Faintly, I could hear the Bull Man rummaging through his sack. He must have been giving

Jake the same choices. "Talk to me, God damn it!" Jake's chains were a wild chorus of clanging metal.

"Be careful, Jake! Is he showing you the items?"

"Yeah! What the ..."

"Jake, don't take anything!"

A bone-chilling silence passed, and I pictured the Bull Man just kneeling there in front of Jake, his big axe buried in the dirt beside him, with the tempting but risky spread laid out before him. Something in my gut told me not to take those items, and I found myself praying desperately for Jake to do the same.

"What do you want from me? Huh?" Jake yelled at the Bull Man.

"Tell me what is happening Jake!"

Jake was a better narrator than I had been when the Bull Man had been on my side. "He is just sitting there like a coward. Why don't you come closer, so I can reach you?" A couple seconds passed, and Jake questioned the man again. "Oh, ok. You want something from me, huh? Come closer then." I pictured the Bull Man extending his hand toward Jake and waiting silently.

I heard Jake's chains rattling again. "You know what? I'm not playing this game."

"Jake? What is he doing?" My heart was racing and my fingers were digging into the stone wall, as if somehow I was going to tear it down and see for myself. The uncertainty was killing me, but in a matter of seconds, all of that stopped cold. Jake's tortured scream was a banshee's shriek shattering the stone wall like a sheet of glass.

My heart skipped and my eyes gaped as I heard his panicked cry. "What the fuck?!" His painful groans melded together with the loathsome grunts of the Bull Man as his feet shuffled around the dirt. I heard what I imagined was Jake on his back, tangled up in his chains and crawling back toward the corner.

"You psycho! What do you want from us?"

"Jake! Are you ok?"

I heard a new sound, something gritty and sharp, like the sound of sharpening a knife on stone.

"No!" Jake yelled. The sharpening sound continued, but began fading, moving away down the tunnel. "What do you want? Come back here! Don't leave me here! Come back!"

"Jake, what happened?"

The grinding sound stopped.

"He stabbed me ... that bastard stabbed me!"

"What? How bad is it? How much are you bleeding?"

"It was my hand, he stabbed me through the hand. Damn it!" I heard him start moving around again. "Oh God, it's bleeding everywhere."

My survival instincts kicked in, and I started thinking clearly again. "Jake, listen, don't panic, it's ok.

Take off your shirt and wrap it tight, stop the bleeding. Pack it with some dirt first. You'll be ok." Somehow, it was easier for me to stay calm when the horror was happening to someone else. Maybe it was the big sister in me.

It sounded like he was doing as I told him, all the while mumbling to himself, though I couldn't make out anything he was saying. Closing my eyes, I let my hands relax and fall into the dirt, where I rested on all fours. For all my effort, I just couldn't imagine how we got here or who had brought us. I tried to think about the party again, but everything was sort of vague, like a faceless person in a weird dream. Too much was distracting my mind. The memories were locked in there somewhere, just beyond the periphery of my thoughts, but it was just too much right now.

"Lani?" Jake called out.

"I'm here."

"You were right."

"What do you mean?"

"I took the water."

6

Some three or four hours later, I had no idea how long really, the Bull Man returned to my side of the tunnel. He greeted me with his usual primal introduction as he stampeded out of the darkness, stopping just outside of reach of my chains. Like before, he slammed his axe into the ground and carefully unloaded his sack, placing vital survival items one by one on a canvas mat in front of me. I was still scared as hell, but it was different this time. I was able to stay more composed, think a little more clearly. This time, I had the knowledge that as long as I didn't touch any of the items, he wouldn't hurt me. At least, I hoped not.

Jake was taunting the Bull Man. "Hey you stupid asshole, why don't you come back over here? Leave Lani alone, come mess with me."

I started tuning Jake out, choosing instead to hyperfocus on the Bull Man, trying to sear every detail about him I could into my memory. Every inch of him would be burned into my brain and when I got out of here he would have no chance of eluding capture.

He was just staring at me, waiting for me to make the same mistake Jake had. Too bad I couldn't see his face. As I examined his hollow black eyes and tough bony snout, I realized that it was a real bull's head. Definitely not a costume. This was a man wearing an actual bull's head. How messed up would he have to be to do all of this? I knew at that moment, more than ever, that this was no ordinary kidnapper. If I didn't get out of here soon, something really depraved was going to happen.

Just like before, when I didn't take the items on the canvas in front of me, the Bull Man loaded everything back into the sack and disappeared down the tunnel. Relief poured over me—then a twinge of anxiety as I felt the dryness in my throat. If I didn't escape soon, I wouldn't have a choice but to take that water. The thought of being stabbed terrified me so bad I had to block it out.

"Lani? You ok?" Jake asked. I didn't answer right away. "Lani?" he repeated.

"Yeah, I'm ok. You?"

"I'm fine."

"How's your hand?"

"Still hurts, but it's not so bad."

"Good."

There was a sort of long, awkward silence at that moment. I think neither of us really knew what else to say. If Jake was feeling like I was, he probably had his back to the wall, his head against the cold stone, and his mind going a mile a minute trying to make sense of everything.

Who did this? How did they get us? Why couldn't we remember? Bits and pieces of it were coming back to me, at least. I had remembered that I left the party with Sami, Ginny, and a guy Ginny had been going on with named Tiago. We were in Sami's car ... Oh yeah! We went back to my apartment after. So it probably wasn't the creepy guy who commented on my lipstick, because we had seen him at my dad's place. Maybe that also meant that whoever got me didn't get Ginny. I really hoped so.

"Lani?" Jake interrupted my thoughts.

"Yeah?"

"What do you remember about the party?"

Weird. It was like he was reading my mind.

"A lot of it's coming back to me. Do you think that someone from the party did this?"

"I don't remember leaving, do you?"

Jake saying that triggered another memory: we were playing beer pong, and Jake was flirting with me. I could picture his face, then I remembered Sami coming up to us and Jake was so peeved. Maybe it was better if I didn't remind him that I left the party with Sami. Although would something like that matter in our situation? I wasn't sure, but it still seemed like something to omit for the time being.

I chose a different detail to divulge instead. "It started raining, right? I think that was around the time I left, but I can't remember much after that. I feel like I'd certainly remember if I got abducted. Do you think someone drugged us?"

"Maybe something was in our drinks."

"It must have been."

What I still couldn't decide was why it was Jake and me. One or the other would make sense, but why the two of us together? We were practically strangers. It would have made more sense to me if the Bull Man had drugged Ginny or Sami instead of Jake. Not that I wanted that. Like I already said, I was praying that they weren't there. But it just seemed so random.

"Tell me what you remember, and I'll tell you what I recall, and maybe we can figure out when someone drugged us."

I suddenly felt angry with Jake for distracting me. "You know what, actually? That doesn't matter right now. We should be focusing on how to escape."

"I agree, but also, we can't do anything right now."

Can't do anything? That was what quitters said. My dad used to tell me that whenever I would try to skimp on lacrosse practice. Rain or shine, mud or grime, sickness or fatigue, you never stop giving it your all. That was what champions were made of. No one was going to do it for me. If I wanted to be a great lacrosse player, I would have to earn it each and every day. My dad used to say the same thing about school, and work, and pretty much everything else. Thanks to him I was a fighter, and I wasn't about to accept that we couldn't do anything. Not until I took my last breath, and trust me: that breath wasn't going to be in this place.

"That's not true," I argued, standing up and hustling around my chain block with renewed motivation. There had to be some way to escape. "We can do *something*, we just don't know what it is yet. We need to keep trying."

"Well, ok, I don't know about you, but I'm fresh out of things to do with dirt, rocks, and chains."

He was frustrated. Couldn't say I blamed him. I was frustrated too, especially because he wasn't wrong. At that moment I was out of ideas as well, feeling around in the dark and touching the same repetitive features in my little dungeon corner. There had to be an answer somewhere, but at the time, it felt like contemplating string theory. Whatever that answer was, it was beyond the scope of my imagination.

"I'm sorry ... I just ... we need to get out of here."

"I know. We will, I promise." I could hear the sincerity in his voice. He was trying to stay positive, which I really appreciated. I found myself smiling for a brief moment. "Now, what do you remember about the party?"

7

By the time Ginny and I had arrived at Cole Diamante's house at seven p.m., the party was already raging. There must have been at least a hundred people there. It was one of those huge, early nineteenth-century style houses, red brick with white trim and huge columns ascending all sides. Black wrought iron fencing entangled with green leafy vines encased the gardens on either side of the front entrance. Two impressive doors with intricate designs of clouded glass and trims of rustic, golden brass kept watch atop a brick staircase, inviting only the worthy to enter. The worthy or, in another case, two hot girls.

Ginny was slightly ahead, hanging on Cole's friend Tiago's shoulder and laughing herself hunched over. I looked back at the other two guys who had met us at the iron gates guarding the entrance from the driveway, and they were taking their time coming up the stone walkway, rippin' a joint. I think one of them was Jimmy, a guy I knew from Applied Physics. He didn't seem to recognize me. Well, except my ass. Looked like he recognized that well enough.

Seeming to realize I'd busted him, Jimmy took the joint from between his lips and extended it toward me, as if that was his intention all along, and exhaled a pungent cloud of smoke in my direction.

"Thanks," I said, grabbing it and taking a hit. Instantly, I coughed it out and shoved it back toward him. "Yo, that's nasty. You on a budget or something?" There was something really off with that weed. I don't know what he paid for it, but it was too much.

"Nah," Jimmy said. "You smoke much?" His friend and I shared an incredulous glance. I could tell he knew it was crap weed as well.

"Yeah, I do, and that stuff is shit," I replied. Jimmy laughed and took another hit before passing it to his buddy.

Ginny was still giggling ahead of me as I turned around. "Are you serious? T, come on," she laughed.

Tiago reached around Ginny's waist and slid his hand smoothly across her back as she went up the stairs. "Girl, I am just saying ... it don't have to be like that." It had been a couple of weeks at least that Ginny had been playing coy with this Tiago guy. The way she was acting, it was probably the night. Good for her; he was hot and totally cool.

Tiago opened the doors and the five of us stepped into the foyer of the plantation, a grand, open room with two staircases lined with white balustrades on either side that curved into a second story balcony. The music was blaring throughout the house and people were dancing and weaving around each other from room to room.

"Yo! T, what up bro?" someone called from across the room.

Tiago acknowledged him and we started scuttling through the crowd. We had barely gotten out of the entryway when the big man Cole appeared from the crowd to greet us.

"Hey, girls, glad you could make it. Lookin' fine this evening," he said.

"Aww, thanks," Ginny replied.

"Nice place," I said. "Why even go to college?"

Cole laughed while he motioned one of his friends over. "Ah, I know. My parents said I need to learn the value of hard work." A moment later, Cole's friend appeared with two beers and handed one each to Ginny and me.

"Thanks. Bottle opener?" I swirled the beer around by the neck.

"Shit." The guy scratched his head. "Hold on."

"Oh, here," Tiago said, grabbing Ginny's beer. Flipping out his lighter, he jammed it up under the cap and popped it off with apparent ease. Triumphantly, he handed the drink back to an easily impressed Ginny and offered to do mine. I let him have his showmanship, and Ginny and I held up our beers before tipping the bottles back and taking the first sip of the evening.

"Thanks, hun," Ginny said, looking Tiago up and

down, adjusting her body to give him a little strut of herself as well. I remember, for the briefest second, being jealous of Ginny. Here was this cut, sexy man, with his arm half-sleeved in tattoos and his dreadlocks, his shiny football ring, and his flashy watch, fawning over her. Ginny always had her hooks in whoever she was fishing for. Then I remembered that I could do that too, it just didn't interest me as much.

"Come on out back," Cole offered. "We got a bar out by the pool."

"Sounds fun. Come on T, let's get it," Ginny said, tugging on his wrist.

Tiago was shouting something over to his friends and when he felt Ginny's hand, he spun back around. "Hold on, babygirl."

Glancing across the crowd, I saw the guys Tiago was talking to, a couple of show-off upper classmen I had seen at some lacrosse games. Guys I had no interest in hanging out with.

"Fuck them," I said. "Let's go, Ginny." My sister agreed and we left Tiago and his buddies in the dust. If he wanted her, he'd catch up.

Outside, the music faded to a comfortable volume and the party guests fanned out across the stone patio and the surrounding lawn. At the edge of the patio, a huge in-ground pool stretched out into the yard in a sort of teardrop shape. There were big rocks on one edge of it and a little stream of water flowing down the center of them into the pool. A solitary willow tree stood watch over the area beside the pool.

"Wow, you know how to throw a party, Cole, I'll give you that," I said as I admired the yard.

"Right? Well, I can't take all the credit. You girls met my buddy?"

"Maybe." Ginny shrugged shyly. "I meet a lot of people."

On cue, Cole tapped some guy's shoulder and he spun around to greet us. "Oh, hey, where'd you go?"

"Had to piss. Hey, you met these girls before? This is Lani, and her sister Ginny," Cole introduced us.

With a quick wave of his hand, the guy said, "Jake. Nice to meet you. Oh, Lani, hey."

"Nice to meet you," Ginny said.

"You two know each other?" Cole asked.

"We have a class together," I said. When Jake looked over at me, he seemed to linger for a second, considering the space beneath the gold ring on my dress. Though it was the intended result of my chosen outfit, I found myself shifting uncomfortably and pulling my dress up an inch. Sorry, but Jake was not my type. He was a nice enough guy, but we didn't seem to have much in common the few times I'd interacted with him. Plus, he seemed a little too eager. I kind of like the chase, to be honest. And his cologne was way too strong.

"I think we met before, too," Jake said, directing his attention back to Ginny.

"Oh really? Yeah, you look familiar."

Cole cut back in. "Well anyway, we were about to play some beer pong when you showed up. You play?"

I was about to say no when Ginny's excited voice overruled me. "Sounds like fun!"

Reluctantly, I agreed. "Ok, cool." It wasn't that I didn't like beer pong, but I didn't want to play with those guys. But Jake was Cole's bestie and Cole was the one who had invited us, so I reasoned that it would be rude not to play a game or two with them.

"Great. The table is over this way."

As we followed Cole down a small set of steps, Tiago emerged from the house. "Hey, Ginny, where you goin' girl?"

"Playing beer pong. Come with us."

"The more the merrier," a seemingly unsure Cole said.

Tiago hustled up to us as we went around the side of the house, where the brick masonry from the back entryway extended into a large rectangular area decorated with patio furniture, standing lanterns, and potted plant life. On one side, the furniture had been pushed aside to set up a wooden table topped with plastic cups. People gathered around the area, sipping mixed drinks and having a great time. Beyond the patio a little way, some people were tossing axes at a pair of wooden targets, something I had always wanted to try. Maybe not around a bunch of drunk college kids, though.

As we approached the table, Cole stepped up between the guys on one side and put his hands on their shoulders. "Hey, we are playin' now, eh?"

"Hold on, we are almost done," one guy responded.

"You guys played already. It's my house. You don't like it, get out."

One of the little plastic ping pong balls bounced off the table and plopped precisely into one of the remaining four cups on Cole's side of the table, causing the other team to taunt the guys wildly, pointing and laughing at them. Annoyed, one guy cursed under his breath, brushed off Cole's hand, and walked away from the table. His buddy grabbed his beer off one of the patio tables and hustled after him.

"Good game ya'll," Cole said to the others. "Our turn now."

"We won anyway," a tall skinny blonde in a dark blue bikini said to her boyfriend as they backed away from the table.

"So, what? Guys versus girls?" Ginny asked.

"Nah," Jake said. "I gotta whoop this man's ass at least once tonight. Lani, you with me, ok?" Oh great. I had to stand next to his cologne for the entire game.

Hopefully I didn't get a migraine from it. It would've been rude to say no.

Hiding my disgust, I put on my best flirty smile and agreed. "Yeah, ok, let's do it."

Cole turned to Ginny and became visibly annoyed as Tiago slid his arms around her waist and leaned into her ear. He whispered something and Ginny covered her mouth and giggled. Tiago tipped back his beer and shot a cocky look at Cole.

"Ginny," I said, trying to keep the party fouls at a minimum. "You playing?"

"Oh, yeah, sorry!" She fumbled around looking for a place to put her beer. Settling on the edge of the table, she bounced up next to Cole and leaned on the table. "Ok, you ready, partner?"

Cole's smile returned and he started to rack the cups in the shape of a pyramid. "You bet. My friend talks a lot of smack, but he sucks at beer pong."

"Dude, you suck at literally everything," Jake countered.

"What about you? You can beat your sister, right?" Cole said to Ginny.

"Easily! Sorry sis," Ginny teased, making a silly face at me.

I flipped the two of them off. "We'll see." I took a quick swig of my beer and eyed Cole and his cocky movements. Honestly, he wasn't a bad guy, but something was rubbing me the wrong way about him right then. Maybe he had been drinking too much or something. He just seemed different than he had been at school.

"Hey, I'm gonna grab another drink, you want something?" Tiago asked.

Ginny lit up and leaned around Cole. "Yes please! Something a little harder."

"Lani?"

"I'm good," I replied.

Tiago disappeared into the house, finally the cups were racked, and the game started.

Right off the bat, Ginny sank one in the middle of our rack. "Ha! First try! Told you sis, you are going down," she declared. I gave her a playful grimace.

Cole missed his shot and Jake taunted him, "Come on bro, what was that?"

"Warm up shot," Cole joked, tipping his beer back nonchalantly.

I took the opportunity to bounce a ping pong ball toward Cole's side of the table and sank it perfectly. "Two cups!" I bragged, pointing at Cole as obnoxiously as I could manage.

"Dude, pay attention!" Ginny scolded him while slapping his shoulder, much to Jake's amusement.

The game went on like that for a few more turns. I was about to make a shot when I heard someone call my name. I turned to see who it was and I immediately froze.

Sami Hyoung was walking beside Tiago, coming toward me, that awkward, sexy smile on his face. And those arms, man. I bet he could lift a car if he had to.

"I guess you made it after all huh?" Sami said as he and Tiago reached the table.

"I guess I did."

"Hey man," Jake greeted Sami. "I'm Jake. You're Sami, right? You play men's lacrosse?"

"Yeah, that's right. Nice to meet you, man," Sami said, offering a handshake to his new acquaintance. Of course Jake knew Sami; he probably knew every lacrosse player at our school, with the amount of time he spent trolling around the field before and after practices. He seemed to be friends with a couple of the other players, but I had never really gotten close to him; pretty much for the same reason I didn't want to be close to him now.

"Same," Jake said.

"A few of us are going for a swim," Sami said, returning his attention to me. "Did you bring a swimsuit?"

"Who needs a swimsuit for a pool party?" I joked.

"I know, right?" Sami smiled and motioned toward his definitely not swim shorts.

"Hey, are we playing?" Ginny asked. I made a face. The game was kind of dying out anyway. Everyone seemed to acknowledge that and moved away from the table so the next group could go. "Well, fine, I need another drink."

"I gotchu. There's a drink table by the pool," Tiago said.

"Good game girls," Cole said, scratching the back of his head, then grabbing his beer and wandering off. He seemed to take the hint well enough, but Jake did not.

"Do you want another drink too, Lani?" Jake asked.

Trying not to be awkward, I said, "No thanks, I'm good. Nice playing with you."

"Yeah, you too. I really like hanging out with you." What the hell was he talking about? We didn't "hang out." We weren't "hanging out" now either. Talk about desperation. He was such a weirdo. I looked at Sami and I could tell he was thinking the same thing.

"Anyway, maybe I'll see you at practice Monday?" I was trying to gracefully exit the conversation.

Finally, he caught on. "Yeah, ok ... cool."

"See you around."

"Yeah, you too."

He did this awkward wave thing and went back into his plastic red cup as Sami and I walked away, hustling to catch up to Ginny and Tiago at the poolside bar. I remember feeling a little bit bad, because Jake was pretty obvious about his feelings for me. That was really why he was always hanging around after lacrosse practices, I was certain. But then, I had to remind myself, I didn't need to feel guilty over something like that. It's not like I led him on. I would never do that to someone. I know that sucks; it happened to me once when I was a junior in high school, with this girl on the soccer team, Janessa. Her and her cute ponytail and witty sense of humor, and those legs for days. We hung out a lot, and I don't know, we had this back-and-forth rapport. I thought it was flirting. Actually, I knew it was flirting, but in hindsight I'm not sure if she knew it was. I remember one night we were with a group of friends at Kyle Jenson's place, smoking weed in the barn, and I jokingly asked Janessa if she was bisexual. It sounded natural because we were all kind of high and we were talking about stuff like that, and she just laughed and said no, she was pansexual. So I kept flirting with her and she, I thought, was flirting back. But later that night we were alone, and when I finally came out with it, and tried to kiss her, she told me she had been joking and she didn't like girls. So much about that was messed up—I mean aside from being a tease, she was insulting me by joking about her sexual identity, as if it is something funny to be queer. Later that night, I went home and cried. Partly because I was embarrassed, but mainly because my heart felt fucking empty, like the essence had been sucked right out of it. I remember how bad that hurt and how long it hurt, so I would never do that to another person. No way.

Anyway, my momentary guilt passed by the time we got to the poolside bar.

"What do you like?" Sami asked me.

"Tequila," I replied.

Sami laughed. "Just tequila? Ma'am, what kind of night are we having?"

I smirked, then stood really straight with my hands behind my back. I looked at him with flirtatious eyes and said, "Try to guess my favorite drink."

I slid on my sly smile as I watched him consider the bottles.

"Hmmm. Well, I don't take you as a sangria girl."

"Why?"

"Just a feeling. What about El Diablo? You like ginger beer?"

"Hmm ... it's ok."

"Ok, huh? So, you like something harder? How about the Brave Bull?"

"What's that?" I wondered, impressed by his on-the-spot knowledge of mixology. To be honest, I didn't really have a favorite drink. Just give me something over ice that'll mess my brain up and it's all good. But this was interesting. Or maybe it was just him.

"It's like a Black Russian, but with tequila," he explained.

I giggled and blushed a little. "What's a Black Russian?"

"Doesn't matter." Sami laughed. He started pouring tequila and sour mix into red cups and said, "There's nothing on this table anyway, so you're getting a margarita."

"Oh, ok, well, I feel special now."

"You should. This stuff is straight-up bottom shelf, no frills for you."

"Gets the job done, right?"

"You bet." Sami handed me the cup and held his up to toast. "Cheers." We touched our cups together and tipped back the first sip of cheap tequila.

"Oh yeah," I commented. "Good stuff."

"Come on, I got a seat over here."

I followed Sami around the edge of the pool toward a group of loungers where he had stacked a couple of towels. There was a little table beside the pool with several empty or half-empty cups, beer bottles, and an ashtray. It was kind of gross, so instead I opted for the ground beside the lounger, set my drink down, and tied my hair back. I grabbed my bikini and considered the water for a minute. Honestly, I wasn't crazy about the pool, just because I didn't want to redo my makeup after, and I wanted to be wearing my sexy underwear if things went the way I wanted with Sami. For a second, it just seemed like a lot of effort. But Ginny was already in, and Sami was going in. I didn't want to be a square, so I smiled at Sami and said, "Be back in two seconds, 'kay?"

"I'm timing you," he joked.

I took off my heels and rushed over to the willow tree, deciding I could slip on my bikini there. Running inside and trying to find the bathroom would take too long, and there was no one over by the tree, so it was totally fine. I did the bottom first, while I still had the dress on, then pulled the dress over my head and switched my top. After I put my underwear into my purse, I hurried back over to Sami.

"That was more than two seconds," he said as I came back to the lounger.

"Shut up," I replied. I was about to say something more, but I got distracted when I saw my phone light up. Flipping open the notification, I saw that my friend Aaron sent me a funny Tik Tok of a dog swimming.

I laughed out loud, and Sami looked over my shoulder and asked, "What?"

Showing him the video, I explained the joke. "I told my friend I was going to a pool party and he sent me this."

He didn't get it, but he laughed anyway. It was funny because I couldn't swim, so I basically look like that in the water.

Someone splashed close to us and the water sprayed up toward me. "Hey!" I yelled, throwing my arm up and raising my leg in defense.

"Come in!" Ginny called to me while swimming on her back.

"Hold on." I looked back at my phone and flipped over to my texts. I don't know why I checked them; there was nothing new. Habit, I guess. I turned around, and Sami had taken his shirt off, giving me incentive to turn my screen off and set my phone on the lounger.

"Hey," I said to Sami. "I never asked you what you like?"

"You mean besides you?"

I blushed a little. "No, what's your favorite drink?"

"I'm not picky. Kinda like you, right?"

"Oh, I'm very picky, actually." I gave him my sly smile again as I tossed my dress over my phone on the lounger. I swiveled toward him a little and added, "And not just with drinks."

He cocked his eyebrow and pretended to be in deep thought for a second, totally not staring at my body, then replied, "So, you're saying my chances of being your friend are slim?"

"You want to be my friend?" I bit my lip a little and smiled playfully. He just smirked and let the silence send his sentiment. Man, he was smooth, but I was enjoying this cat-and-mouse thing we were doing, so I didn't want to come on too strong yet. I held my hands up to my chest, crossed my fingers, and said, "Keep your fingers crossed." Without warning, I pushed my hands out toward Sami's chest and shoved him backward into the pool.

I jumped in after him, and in a moment we both came up from the water, and he started laughing and coming after me.

"Dirty trick!" he yelled, trying to grab my shoulders and push me underwater.

"No!" I kicked my feet and splashed around while I tried to escape. I splashed water in his face, which temporarily stopped him, but he came right back and tackled me into the water. When I came up, I yelled, "You're going down, sir!"

"Ok, try it," he said, treading water and daring me to try to tackle him.

"Don't push me under."

He made a face as he watched me doggy paddling at him. "Wow, you look threatening."

"Shut up!" I laughed. I was kind of embarrassed about him seeing me swim, and even more so that he had made a comment, but I wasn't going to let it ruin my night. I was having way too much fun.

"Hey guys!" Ginny called. "We're playing chicken!"

"Ok!" I answered. I sort of swam into Sami and said, "Carry me."

I grabbed his shoulders and he swam us over to the shallower part of the pool where Ginny, Tiago, and some other people were already starting chicken fights. We joined in and did that for fifteen minutes or so. I fell literally every time, and I'm pretty sure my nose had permanent water up it. After the last fight, I swam over to my drink and realized I was nearly empty.

"Hey, I'm going to get another drink, you guys want some?" I asked the group. A couple people said yes, and I got out of the pool and started around the pool toward the drink table.

As I sauntered up to the bar, it swept over me. I did it. I really did it. I flirted with Sami Hyoung and he flirted back! It felt awesome, knowing I was getting exactly what I wanted. If I had my way, that was going to continue, too. I started picturing it, all of Sami's ripped lacrosse body on top of me, dominating me with all that strength, scooping me up off the sheets and into his powerful embrace. He was just relentless, and I was falling into him, biting his shoulders, shredding his skin with my fingernails. I wanted all the blood and sweat. I wanted to lick it off him. Every second, all night, me and Sami in my bed.

I was still half-lost in my fantasy when someone said, "You makin' drinks?"

I snapped out of it. "Oh! Yeah, sorry." My cheeks went red as I realized I had been just staring at the rows of bottles on the table, two empty cups sitting in front of me. Hopefully this guy wasn't a mind reader. Shaking my head out of my lusty thoughts, I started mixing margaritas. The guy was kind of just staring at me, so I paused and shot back, "Are you making drinks, or what?"

"Rum runner." He smirked, raising his plastic cup toward me. I realized I didn't recognize that guy. Actually

... I wasn't a hundred percent sure whether I did or not. There was something familiar about him, but I couldn't put my finger on it.

Playing it cool, I said, "Ick ... I can't do rum. So, are you a friend of Cole's?"

"But you drink that Mexican piss?"

I glanced at the bottle of Cuervo Gold, then back at him. "It's fine; just tastes like lime and salt. Rum gives me headaches. So, how do you know Cole?"

Leaning back on the brick planter behind him, the guy avoided my question again. "You drink rum on your twenty-first?"

"What?"

"Drank too much rum or something?"

I gave him a weird look. "No ..."

"You aren't twenty-one, are you? Do you go to Penn State?"

"What are you, a fucking cop?" I sneered. I finished making my drinks and thank God for that. Picking up the cups, I said, "My boyfriend is waiting, sorry. Have a good night."

"You too."

He tipped the cup toward me again as I turned to go. As I was walking off, I heard a couple of girls go up to the bar and he started talking to them too. What a weirdo.

When I got back to the pool, Sami and Tiago were

in the water with some other guys tossing a football back and forth.

"Yo!" Sami laughed, stumbling backward as he tried to avoid the freight train that was Tiago. Sami kind of fell into the water before he was fully tackled, and the football skipped across the water where they went under.

"I got it!" Ginny declared, swimming clumsily over to the fumbled ball.

I laughed at the sight of her trying to swim with the football under her armpit. "Ginny, what are you doing?"

"What do you mean? Come play with us!"

"Hold on." I knelt beside the pool and set our drinks carefully onto the cement, away from the edge. I stretched out one leg and dipped it into the water, and I noticed in the corner of my eye, my phone light up under my dress.

"Lani!" I heard Ginny calling. Behind her, the guys were splashing around and laughing like buffoons. But I was distracted. I don't know why, but I could never not look at a text. No matter what, I had to, or it would bother me all night. So, I pushed my dress aside and went to look at it, but right as I reached for the phone, I felt someone grab my ankle. I yelped as Sami yanked me off the edge of the pool into the water.

Bursting up from beneath the water, I exclaimed, "You asshole!" I started hitting his shoulder and pushing him away as he and Tiago were laughing at me. Part of me actually was annoyed, because I hated being startled, but I got over it quickly.

We went on messing around for a while, tossing the ball, splashing each other, swimming to the edge to pound liquor. It was all so fun, but eventually it started getting really cold. I remember it got a lot darker, and I looked up and noticed the moon was gone, totally covered in clouds black as the night sky. The wind was picking up too, like a thunderstorm or something was about to happen.

"Brr." Ginny was the first to acknowledge what I was thinking, hugging her shoulders and shivering back and forth in the waist-deep water.

I agreed. "Um, yeah, it's fucking cold." Everyone else seemed to be on the bandwagon, as they were all getting out of the pool and drying off. It seemed like a lot of people had either gone inside or left the party altogether. Cole's yard had thinned out quite a bit.

Sami beat me to our little table and lounger where we had all our stuff and passed me my towel as I got out of the water.

"Thank you." I wasted no time wrapping myself up like a cocoon.

"No problem," he said. "Holy crap, it got dark out here."

"Is it supposed to storm?" Ginny wondered.

"I don't know," Tiago said. He took a swig of something out of a red cup and added, "It's cool. You want to dry off and get out of here?"

Sami asked, "You want to go?"

"Yeah, man, I'm hungry. You wanna get Five Guys?"

"I don't know. Ladies, you want to get some burgers?"

"I don't care," I said. "Let's just get out of the wind."

"A'ight, let's go," Sami decided.

We started across the lawn toward the driveway. The whole time, Ginny and Tiago were messing around. I don't know what they were doing—laughing, tripping over each other and whatnot. I remember getting kind of quiet, mostly because I was so cold, and then it got even colder when it started to rain.

For some reason, I couldn't remember anything about Five Guys. Maybe we never went after all. Damn, we must have been drugged. Did roofies make you forget things? I felt like they did, and Jake agreed. We both decided it must have been roofies, because Jake felt the same way as me—like he was slowly putting things together. Initially, he couldn't remember leaving the party, but after my story he recalled that he had left an hour or so after me. He and Cole and some other people had gone inside the house and played Kings for a while.

When Jake was done telling me all this, I felt more confused than before. "Wait ... are you sure that's right? I feel like too much time passed between when we both supposedly left and whenever we got kidnapped. Like, wouldn't the drugs have kicked in?" I wondered,

Jake was silent, probably thinking.

"I mean, think about it," I continued. "We weren't together after the party, right? He had to have gotten us at the party. So, why did it take so long?"

"I don't know, Lani. I just don't know."

There had to be something missing.

What was I missing?

The thought of it was driving me mad, and I had to reset my brain. Plus, I was starting to feel weak from exhaustion and lack of sustenance. For the first time since I had first woken in that hell, I let myself drift off to sleep.

8

If I had to guess, a day or so passed, though it was impossible to be sure. I figured out that the Bull Man would show up roughly every two or three hours, alternating between Jake and me. That time may not have been accurate, but his coming felt pretty routine and that was how I gauged the passage of time. My sense of urgency to escape hadn't waned, but I just couldn't figure out how to do it. And I had to do it soon, because my thirst was becoming dire. In my desperation, I tried all the things again, just to check the boxes. I went at the masonry again to look for weak spots, tried to grind my shackles against the base of the chain to wear it down, and I even dug a hole all the way around the chain block, digging at least six inches into the dirt. I couldn't dig any further; the ground became too rocky. There was no sign of reaching the bottom of that block. I even tried to wriggle my wrists around, bend them in any sort of way to escape the bindings, hoping that maybe I could figure out an angle where I could dislocate them and pop out, even partially. No such luck.

After a while I realized it was, unfortunately, time to take the water. I had to, or I was going to die before I could figure things out. The next time the Bull Man came to my side, I took several deep, hyperventilating breaths and went for it. He grunted when I set my hand on it and I paused momentarily, looking wide-eyed up at him. I noticed his hand wasn't on the axe this time, so maybe he wouldn't kill me. I pulled the water toward me, and a couple seconds passed before the Bull Man reacted. He stood up suddenly, rushed toward me, and grabbed my head, ramming it into the stone wall. It wasn't hard enough to concuss me, but it definitely knocked me down. The shock alone was enough to leave me disoriented. Before I knew what was going on, I felt the Bull Man's massive hand pressing the side of my face against the dirt. I kicked and struggled, but his knee came down on my back and quickly shut me down. The next thing I felt was the cartilage on the top part of my ear ripping as he cut three little slits with his knife. I screamed in agony and surprise while he mutilated me. I never expected such a small cut to hurt so bad. Part of it was mind over matter, I was sure. I mean, I could hear the little layer of cartilage bending, popping, and ripping. The sensory experience of that was so horrific and intense. Never had I been so grateful for anything as when he finally got up off me and began loading his items back into the sack. He left the water bottle for me as my reward for enduring his torture and disappeared back into the darkness with the rest of the items.

    Jake had been calling to me, but I couldn't answer.

All I could do was lay there in shock, bawling my eyes out.

Maybe half a day passed. The Bull Man came and went as usual, except one time: he entered my tunnel and went about his usual brokering of items across the canvas. Only this time, when I refused to take any of the items, he took the little piece of paper with the question mark on it and held it before me between two of his grimy fingers. After displaying it for a few seconds, he slowly unfolded it, bit by bit, making an emphatic chorus out of the crinkling noises.

I waited anxiously as he unfolded that mysterious paper, and when he was finally done, my eyes followed the paper as he set it on the ground in front of me. In the orange glow of the Bull Man's lantern, I could make out one sentence written on the paper:

I'm closer than you think.

He let me stare at it for a moment, then loaded his items back into the sack and retreated into the blackness once more.

I'm closer than you think. What did it mean?

I called to Jake, "Hey! He gave me something!"

"Really? What is it?" Jake asked.

"A piece of paper."

"The one with the question mark?"

"Yeah."

"What's on it?"

"It says 'I'm closer than you think,'" I told him.

Naturally, Jake had the same question as me. "What does that mean?" I was about to reply, but he added, "Never mind. Fuck him. It's all part of his game. Forget about it, Lani. He's just messing with you."

I knew Jake was probably right, but at the same time, I didn't want to rule out any possibilities. More than one thing could be true. The Bull Man could have been messing with me, but I was certain the phrase he had written on that paper was not entirely random. If it was a game, and we weren't dead yet, maybe that meant there was a way to win. Whatever it was, I was determined to find it.

Patrick Carpenter

I'm closer than you think.

What the fuck ...

9

The creepiest event of the entire night had happened long after the party. I hadn't told Jake this part before, when we were talking about the party, but Sami and I had gone back to my place. As I sat in silence, I recounted those moments over and over, and I thought I had a pretty clear idea of the timeline now.

We had all gone inside real quick to finish drying off and say goodbye. Cole wasn't around and I wasn't up for looking for him. Instead, I ducked into the bathroom for a minute to change and put on my makeup. The whole time I was in there, some fuckin' guy was pounding on the door, saying he had to piss. I kept saying I'd be right out, but two seconds later, he'd be pounding away. Annoyed, I decided to do my makeup in the car, and just finished changing and shoved open the door, pushing past the drunken idiot outside. I found Ginny, and there was still no sign of Cole, so we all decided to just leave.

After we stumbled out of Cole Diamante's house, me, Ginny, Sami, and Tiago were walking across the front lawn. Everyone was pretty drunk, and we were trying to work out who was the most fit to drive (although really, none of us were).

"You good to drive?" I asked Sami.

"Oh yeah," Sami promised. "Only had a couple beers. You bring your car?"

"Nah, we came in Ginny's."

Looking over his shoulder, Sami called back to her, "Ginny! You cool with leaving your car?"

"What?" she asked, seeming to only partially engage him.

Tiago playfully rapped her shoulder. "Yo, he's askin' you something."

"I know, asshole."

"Ginny," I said, getting slightly annoyed. "How are we gonna get your car in the morning?"

"Oh, I don't know. We'll ask Dad to borrow his car."

"I can bring you, baby. No worries," Tiago offered.

"So ... we're good?" Sami asked.

"Yeah, yeah, we good," Tiago said.

I rolled my eyes. "You guys are fuckin' drunk." Although, I wasn't too sober myself. I had only two margaritas and a couple of hard seltzers, so I'm not sure why I felt so tipsy. Then again, I hadn't eaten, and I drank everything in less than two hours. So I guess that was why.

We got to Sami's car, and I was instantly impressed by the sleek polished maroon and low snub-nosed body style of the Camaro. "Wow, nice car. I haven't seen one of these a long time," I commented.

"Yeah, thanks. It was my dad's," he said as he opened the passenger door for me.

"Thank you, what a gentleman," I said, slipping into the seat. "What is it, a ninety-three?"

"You're welcome. And yeah, Z28," he replied before carefully closing my door and heading around the other side.

Tiago and Ginny fell into the back seat. Ginny was giggling and acting like an idiot, and Tiago was saying something to her, but honestly, I don't remember what, because it was so loud in there. Sami got in, started the car, and got the heat going. Thank God; with the rain picking up it was uncomfortably cold.

"So, you into cars?" Sami asked, leaning toward me a little with one hand slung over the steering wheel and the other on the stick.

"Kinda. I used to help my dad rebuild his Pontiac."

"Oh yeah? Seventies muscle? Does he race?"

"No. My uncle used to do that, and my dad helped him build, but he never raced. Do you?"

Before he could answer, someone yelled across the lawn, "Hey!"

"Who's that?" I wondered.

"Yo, we goin' or what?" Tiago leaned up to the center console.

Sami waved his hand in Tiago's face and said,

"Hold on." Leaning out his window, Sami called back to the guy, who was coming across the lawn, "Hey! What's up?"

As he got closer, Cole's lanky figure came into view. Right behind him was body-spray Jake.

"Oh great, this guy," I lamented. The last thing I wanted was for him to see me and Ginny leaving his party with Sami and Tiago. Not that I owed him anything, or Ginny either, but it was pretty obvious why he invited us there and I just didn't want to rub it in his face.

Cole was nearly at Sami's window when he asked, "You guys leaving already?"

"Yeah, man, we are getting Five Guys," Sami told him. "Great party, though, for real."

"Yeah, thanks for inviting us," Ginny added.

"Oh, my pleasure," Cole said, now beside Sami's window, leaning on the idling Camaro. "Nice car, man."

"Thanks," Sami said.

"A bunch of us went inside; we are gonna play Kings if you guys wanna chill a little longer." As he finished his pitch, he looked inside, specifically at me, and cracked a drunken smile. I sank into my seat, trying to let Sami's body block as much of me as possible, and pulled my dress up an inch.

"Thanks, man, but we are heading out," Sami declined. Thank the lord. If he had said yes to going back inside, I would have been so pissed.

"Ok, well, thanks for coming. Be safe out there ... lots of crazies out tonight."

"See you at school."

Cole nodded and eased himself off the vehicle. Jake, who had stayed a few feet behind him, sipping on his little red cup, did an awkward two-finger wave and followed Cole back up the lawn. Sami put the car in gear and pulled off the curb. As we started down the road, a sudden realization came over me, dropping a ball of nerves into the pit of my stomach. Sami was driving us home, and more specifically, he was driving *me* home, and at some point, I was going to be alone with him. Was I going to invite him in when we got back to my place? That's what I wanted, right? It was; that's why I bothered to change clothes, but all the sudden, I was nervous as hell about it.

"You guys good?" Sami asked, looking quickly over his shoulder at the two in the back, who were making a ruckus and moving around the seats. When he looked back, he flicked on the radio and some hip-hop song started playing.

"Yeah, yeah," Ginny said, settling into her seat.

"Eww." I scoffed at the music and immediately began flipping through the channels.

"Yeah, put on whatever you want," Sami said. We started driving along, and I got my iPhone synched to his Bluetooth and put on Adventure Club. Ginny and Tiago were still laughing and bouncing around the back seat. Sami smiled and said to me, "You like this music?"

"What, you don't?" I replied. "Don't tell me you like that garbage you had on."

"Hey, I'll tell you what, Tupac is real hip-hop. None of that bebop bullshit they got now."

"Oooh, is that true hip-hop? Please, tell me more."

"Well, it's about the pain, right? The emotions of oppression, not flash and bling. It just doesn't feel as real now, you know?"

"Not really," I laughed. "So, do you feel oppressed, is that it?" As we kept talking, I pulled down the overhead mirror, grabbed my lipstick from my bag, and began carefully touching myself up. Good thing too; I looked a little scary after the pool and the rain.

Sami smiled playfully and said, "Nah, girl. Actually, I'm feelin' pretty blessed, to be honest."

"Wow, ok, you corny as fuck, dude," I heard Ginny say.

"Who, me?" Sami asked, looking over his shoulder for a brief second. It was just enough for him to swerve, then suddenly jerk the wheel back as he realized he was over the center line.

"Yo!" I yelled as I smudged my lipstick. "Not cool."

"Sorry," he said.

"Hey, we're up here on the left," Tiago said, thankfully preventing any awkwardness from happening.

"Here?" Sami asked. "You don't wanna go get food?"

"Nah, yellow one. We good, just drop us here." Ginny was laughing and crawling over Tiago, and she accidently kicked the back of my seat while doing it, disrupting my makeup routine for the second time. Thankfully, I had the mascara in my hand, but not actually on my lashes yet.

"Ginny! For fuck's sake!" I yelled at her. My sister could be such a sloppy drunk.

We finally pulled up to the house and my sister and her beau got out. We waited until they were inside before Sami pulled off the curb. The thing I remember most about that moment was the nerves, the pit in my stomach that just materialized from nowhere as soon as I realized I was alone with Sami. And I knew what was going to happen next. I definitely wanted it; I had wanted it before I went to that party, but now that it was here my heart was pounding.

"How you feelin'?" he asked me while we sat at the stoplight down the road.

"Fine, you?"

"I barely drank," he laughed.

"I know, you prude."

"Prude? Who, me?"

"No one else in this car."

"Haha, whatever." He paused for a moment, and at

the next light he asked, "Your place is up here, right?"

"Yeah, on the left."

"Ok. So, you have fun tonight?"

"Definitely."

Sami pulled up to the curb and shifted the car into park. "So did I."

I let him linger for a couple seconds as our gaze met, curious to see if he would make the first move. When he didn't, I took matters into my own hands.

Leaning toward him and sort of laughing about it, I said, "I feel like the night's not over, I don't know."

A victorious smile formed on Sami's face as he hit the button next to the steering wheel and turned the car off. I smiled at him and stumbled my way out of the car and around the curb. Sami caught me as I tripped a little and we laughed it off on our way up the walkway.

"You need another one?" Sami joked.

"Why, you got some?"

"What?"

"Nah, I'm good," I laughed. I had no idea what we were even talking about.

We were at the front door now, and I was standing one stair above Sami, digging for my house key in my little purse. Somehow, I still fit a lifetime of shit in that tiny thing. It was a talent.

"You sure you're good?" he asked, his eyebrows raised amusedly as he watched me fumble about.

"Oh, crap!" I exclaimed as I dropped my lip gloss into the bush beside the front door.

I went to bend over the railing for it, but Sami tapped my shoulder. "I got it."

"Sorry. I'm an idiot." I went back to my purse as Sami rummaged around the bush, this time finding my keys easily. "Got 'em!" I unlocked the front door.

"Here you go," he said, coming back around the railing and handing me the lip gloss. He rubbed his neck and looked down a little, then back at me, all awkward and cute. He was trying to figure out how to ask if I wanted him to come in, if that was what my comment in the car had meant. It totally was, but I was curious what he'd say, so I just looked at him. A couple seconds passed, and he said, "Well, if you want me to come in, you'll have to invite me. I'm a gentleman, ma'am." He got this glint in his eye and a pretty little grin, like he knew he was in.

I left him on the hook for a couple seconds, scrunching my face very inquisitively, then I laughed out loud. "Are you serious? Sir, I am a lady. I don't know what you thought."

"True," he replied, advancing up the stairs. I felt his hands glide across my hips and up to my lower back as he pressed into me. I didn't fight it. "But no one else is here to judge. So, who cares?" My stomach got that pit feeling again, but this time it was from excitement and anticipation, that feeling of taking a leap and surrendering to the vulnerability of the moment. He leaned in to kiss me and my whole body felt weak for just a moment. My arms found their way around his body, and I closed my eyes and let myself fall into him.

We were all over each other, and before long, we were stumbling through my front door and knocking things over as we threw each other across the walls. God, it was so hot. I felt like a ragdoll, in the best way. We were literally knocking stuff over, like they do in movies. His intense, powerful body was coming at me exactly the way I'd imagined, and I was loving every second of it.

At the bottom of the stairs Sami lifted me up against the wall, kissing me passionately and thrusting his body against me. I wrapped my legs around him and bit his lip. He pulled away for a second and I teased him, "Hmm ... not very gentleman-like, sir."

"Oh, sorry. I can stop if you want," he said in a joking tone.

I smiled and started making out with him again. He kissed my neck a couple times, and that was it. I was done waiting.

"Carry me," I ordered him.

"Huh?"

"Carry me."

Sami looked at the stairs and seemed to understand. He smirked, then pulled me up onto his shoulder and started up the stairs.

Caught off guard, I started kicking my feet, both laughing and screaming. "Oh my God! What are you doing?"

"You said carry you."

"Not like a sack of potatoes, dummy!"

He laughed and picked up the pace until we got to the upstairs hallway, where he stopped and considered the doors on either side of us.

"Put me down! The blood is rushing to my head!" I said, pounding on his back and dying laughing at the silliness of it.

Sami pulled me down from his shoulder, so he had me laid across his hands in front of him. "Which one?" he asked.

I pointed to the left.

Sami carried me into my bedroom and over to the bed, where he let me down onto my feet. We made out for a few seconds, and he started taking off my dress. My body felt so hot, like our passion was raising my body temperature. It's cliché, but my knees felt weak as he was taking my clothes off and touching my body. When I was totally naked except my black lace underwear, I guided his hand to my breast and pushed myself into him. We kissed again, and I bit him harder this time. He replied by moving his hands down my torso and scooping me up onto the bed. I watched him pull his shirt off his gorgeous body before he came back down toward me, kissing me and touching me and driving me wild.

I was lying there, lost in the moment, as he started slowly moving down my body, toward the foot of the bed. My bed was positioned on the wall adjacent to the door, and the headboard itself was in view of the doorway, so I could see down the upstairs hallway, all the way to my roommate's door on the other side. As I was laying there, feeling him kiss my stomach, eagerly waiting for what came next, I turned my head.

There was someone standing in the hallway, watching me.

"Oh my God!" I screamed, jumping up and pulling the pillows over my naked body.

"What? What did I do?" Sami asked in a panic and reached for my shoulder to console me.

"Who the fuck are you?!" I demanded. The dude was modest height and boxy shaped, and he was dressed in full fisherman attire, from the gray rubber boots to the long, dusty brown raincoat and floppy hat. I couldn't see his face because of the dark. What the hell was he doing in my house?

"Lani! Lani, who are you talking about?"

I pointed frantically, but the man booked it down the stairs before Sami caught sight of him.

"He ran down the stairs! He was right there, a big fucking man in a fisherman's outfit!" I started bawling so hard as I told him about it. I thought my heart was going to explode, I was so scared.

"Whoa, wait, you saw a man in the hallway?"

"Yes, I swear!"

"Ok, ok. I'll check it out."

"Wait," I pleaded, grabbing his arm as he slid off the bed. "Behind the nightstand, get my bat."

Sami reached for the old metal bat between my nightstand and my headboard and made for the door. While he did so, I opened my purse and grabbed my pepper spray. I rushed out of bed, wrapped myself in my fluffy white robe off the back of the door, and clutched Sami's arm as we ventured into the dark hallway.

I reached for the light switch, but Sami swatted me away. "Shh, I'm gonna surprise this asshole," he explained. I went along with it, even though every part of me was urging me not to continue. This was the same mistake they made in every horror movie ever. When something goes bump in the night, you don't chase it in the dark. No, sir. That's how you get murdered. But honestly, I was too scared to object, just as long as Sami was in the front.

We rounded the corner and began to slowly descend the stairs. Sami was being extra careful, which was great, because those stupid stairs were so old and creaky. If we started with all that noise, it would be totally irrelevant that we were shrouded in darkness.

When we came to the base of the stairs, there

were two possible ways to go—to the left into the living room, or to the right, down the narrow hallway into the kitchen, where the front door was. I knew which way I wanted to go: out that door as fast as humanly possible, but not unless I knew for sure the coast was clear.

Sami stopped on the bottom step, pressing his back against the wall, and urged me to stay where I was. He gripped the steel handle with both hands and swung himself around the corner, ready to smash the intruder if he was waiting for us.

Nothing.

I watched nervously as Sami checked the hallway. He came back to the base of the stairs and whispered to me, "Lani."

"What?"

He tilted his head down the hall. "The front door."

I peered around the corner, and sure enough, the door was wide open. I could smell the fresh rain and feel the cool evening breeze funneling down the hallway toward us.

"Did he leave?"

"I don't know."

"What should we do?" I asked, still refusing to leave the safety of the bottom step. Just because the door was open didn't mean he was gone. That creep could have done that to throw us off, then as soon as we let our guard down, he would jump out of a closet or something and stab us to death.

"I'm calling the cops," Sami decided.

"Ok, yeah. Oh my God, who was that guy? Sami! Who was he?"

"I don't know, but you should call. I'll keep watch. Plus, you saw him, right? You can tell the cops who to look for."

"Good idea."

I remembered scattered bits of what happened after that. I know the cops showed up about twenty minutes after that. Good thing we weren't actively being murdered, because seriously, twenty minutes? When they arrived, I recounted the story the best I could for the police. I remember thinking that they didn't believe me. Sami never saw anyone, only I did. And what was really strange was that the cops claimed there were no signs of forced entry, no tracks, no evidence whatsoever that anyone other than Sami and I had been in the house. They said they would leave an officer parked outside overnight, just in case, but I could tell they thought I was seeing things or having a bad dream or whatever.

It was weird, though—whenever I picture that moment when the fisherman guy appeared, it was just really off. Maybe my brain confused things because I was in shock, I don't know. I also remembered feeling super lightheaded too, so maybe my mind was playing tricks on me. But whatever the reason, when I pictured him standing there, the spot where he was didn't make sense. Like, where it was, he would have been standing inside the railing, beyond the stairs. When I pictured what happened next, I could see him dashing down the stairs, only I don't hear any footsteps. It looked like he went through the railing. Basically, it didn't make sense. But at the same time, I had forgotten parts of the night leading up to this, so was I confused? Was it because of the drugs? Either way, I know I saw him there. I wasn't crazy.

For a little while after the Bull Man had cut my ear and left me, Jake and I discussed the note. Jake stuck to his guns, insisting the note was meaningless, nothing more than a way to mess with our minds. After thinking it over some more, I was sure the note meant the Bull Man was someone we knew. Whoever he was, he was "closer than we think." Either way, we both agreed that it wasn't important until we figured out how to get out of our chains.

Things went quiet again, and my adrenaline wore off. Giving in to the exhaustion, I fell asleep.

10

"Lani!" I woke up to Jake yelling.

"Huh? Jake?" I called back.

"Lani, I got a key!"

Certain I heard him incorrectly, I replied, "What? A key? Where did you find it?"

"He gave it to me."

"What? I don't understand, did it work?"

"Yeah, I got the chains off."

I was so confused. "Wait, he just gave it to you?"

"It was one of the items this time."

"Oh my God, you took the key from the sack? Jake, what did you give him in return?"

"Nothing, he just let me take it and he disappeared. Lani, I'm gonna come get you, don't worry. We'll be out of here soon."

Something about this seemed off, and I suddenly felt unbearably anxious. Why would the Bull Man give Jake the key? Especially for free. He had stabbed Jake when he had taken the water, and mutilated my ear when I took it. This must have all been part of his game. It was going to happen eventually, somewhere inside the void of darkness beyond these chain blocks.

"Jake, don't go down that tunnel," I heard myself

say. I was still clouded by brain fog, probably from hunger and fatigue, but regardless, when I said that out loud my thoughts made sense. The punishment was pending, ready to be delivered in some yet unseen, unspeakable way.

"What? Lani, are you serious? I'm gonna come get you, then we are getting the hell out of here."

"No, you can't! He will make you pay for that key."

Silence for a moment. I could picture Jake's face twisting with confusion. "What?" he replied.

My breath became labored as I struggled to convey my sense of urgency through the stone wall. "When you took the water, he stabbed you. I took the water and he cut me. He holds out his hand whenever he comes down the tunnel because we are supposed to pay for his things. If he gave you the key, it wasn't for free. Don't you get it? He *wants* you to go down that tunnel, and he is gonna make you pay for it."

"Lani, I'll be ok. Even if you are right, what choice do we have? We'll die if we stay here."

He was going to die down that tunnel, too. I knew he was right; there was no way out where we were, and if he didn't do something, we could die sitting there in those chains, wondering what would have happened if he had gone. But I was right too, and the thought of him leaving me there was too terrifying to bear. If he did die somewhere down there, I'd never know it, and I'd be all alone, waiting for a rescue that would never come. I started to cry as the thought of that began instantly melding into my fear of never seeing my family again, never knowing if Ginny was down there somewhere, or ever getting another chance to tell all of them that I loved them. I wondered if they'd ever find me, and if they did, would I be a chopped up, half-decomposed corpse? Would they find me in some river or washing up on some beach, my limbs poking out of degraded black trash bags? Or maybe my fate in this place was something so bad I hadn't even imagined it yet.

"Lani?" Jake's voice brought me back.

"I'm here," I cried.

"We are gonna get out of here, you hear me?"

"I know. Can you just please be careful? You have the lighter still, right? Look out for traps." I suddenly pictured a horror movie I'd watched once about a serial killer who broke into some person's house and turned the whole place into a deathtrap. In my mind, I could see Jake wandering through the darkness and tripping a wire somewhere, ending up with a spike in his chest or a shotgun blast to the face or something.

"Yeah, I have the lighter and I have the key. If it works on my chain, it'll work on yours. Don't worry, Lani, I'm coming to get you. I promise."

God, I hoped he would keep that promise.

11

After Jake was gone, there was a new sense of dread in that place. It took the form of deathly silence, a quiet so intense I could hear my own heartbeat. Every second I spent dwelling on Jake out there in the darkness I became more and more anxious. I had to take my mind off it.

I drifted back toward the piece of paper the Bull Man had dropped in my tunnel.

I'm closer than you think.

I was still certain that it meant the Bull Man was someone I knew. If he was, I hadn't the faintest idea what the motive would be. Maybe he was just some psycho messing with us, but I wasn't sure. Or perhaps the Bull Man was working with someone I knew. After all, he couldn't be doing it all alone. He came down there every two hours, so when would he have slept? Not to mention, I had no idea how far the tunnel in front of me went or how much effort was involved in bringing us here. The fact that Jake had been gone now for at least an hour and I hadn't heard a trace of him told me there was a whole lot more terror down there than my little chain block.

Contemplating all this, I began trying to form a suspect list.

My parents got divorced two years ago, and it was pretty nasty. Naturally, when I began thinking about bad situations and questionable motives, my mind went there. It was in early October when my dad was supposed to be working in Saxton fifty minutes or so from our home, and he wasn't going to be back until after supper. Well, later that day, for some reason that my dad never told me, he came home early, and he caught my mom with some scumbag in their own bed. I mean, of all the places my mom could have had an affair, doing it there was probably the most insulting. I think she did it on purpose, to spite my dad, because she was like that. When my mom got mad, she could be hella scary. And as I would later learn, she was big mad at my dad. So she fucked a stranger in the bed on purpose, no doubt about it. Maybe she even wanted to get caught, I don't know. I do think my dad suspected it though, which is probably why he came home early. I wasn't totally sure. My dad shielded us from a lot of that, which was good on his part.

My mom dragged out the divorce for months, and when it was done, she went off the rails. Like I said, when she got mad, she got crazy. She had churned through a few more scumbags since then, too. Part of me wondered if she was always like that, and if she was, how my dad ended up with her. Anyway, for a split second, I was picturing my mom's boyfriend, the one from the affair, and wondering if he would do something like this. He had lingered for a while, on and off with my mom, and I know he was abusive toward her. He'd probably chain someone up. But no, that thought was dismissed almost instantly. It was just too maniacal, even for someone like him. This situation, this dungeon, it wasn't normal at all. Whoever did this had to be super deranged.

I started considering other options. I didn't have any enemies that I knew of. Except maybe ... there was this lacrosse coach on campus who was a pretty grabby guy. He was always touching the girls more than he needed to when it came to stretching and stuff. One time, he was getting like that with me and I called him out. *Like, bro, your hand is literally on my ass. Pretty sure I can flush my own legs, thanks.* It was all awkward after that, but thankfully it didn't last long, because I showed up to practice a week later and he was gone. I found out another girl had reported him for soliciting sexual favors in exchange for field time. The guy was a serious scumbag. Maybe it was him, kidnapping girls and chaining them up. But if that was the case, why Jake? Maybe he thought Jake was my boyfriend and it made him angry. It wouldn't have been a farfetched guess; Jake was always hanging around the lacrosse field and talking to me after practice. Looking back, it was pretty obvious that Jake was into me well before Cole's party, but he just wasn't my type. I felt bad now, thinking about Jake braving the dark of the tunnels to try and save us, and I had never given him the time of day.

Honestly, I just couldn't picture anyone I knew doing this.

An hour or so passed and the Bull Man came once more. He laid his usual canvas across the dirt in front of me, only this time he placed a copper key among the items. Finally, I could get out of these chains! Thankfully Jake had taken the key first, so I was confident it would be ok. Whatever tribulations lay beyond the darkness of this tunnel was another thing; at the moment all I cared about was being free to move about.

Nervously, I considered it for another moment, trying to discern any kind of reaction from the Bull Man as I reached toward the key. I felt the smooth copper in my hand. My heart was racing as the Bull Man watched me pull the key away from the spread and get started on my shackles. My hands were so shaky that I missed the keyhole and dropped the key in the dirt. I was fumbling around for the key when I heard the Bull Man snort. I froze, my hand mid-reach, my eyes darting upward.

Without warning, the Bull Man smashed his big, club-like hand over the back of my head, smacking me into the dirt face-first. I screamed as I felt his foot pressing down on my back.

"Please, no, please don't!" I begged. I didn't even

know what he was doing, but whatever it was, I didn't want it.

He released a savage grunt and shifted around so he was behind me. I felt his knee pushing on my shoulders and within seconds I could barely breathe. It felt like he was crushing my diaphragm, and worse, there was a rock right under one of my ribs and he was shoving me into the ground so hard I thought it was going to rip into me.

"I can't ... breathe!" I choked out.

I felt him lean over me as I was struggling to get out from under him, my chains rattling wildly as my arms flailed about in the dirt.

Next, his hand came crashing down onto the back of my head and my face scraped across the coarse ground, back and forth, then up and down, bashing me, dragging me. I choked and coughed hysterically after breathing in a cloud of dust and dirt. I was trying to beg him to stop, but all I had time to do was suck in desperate breaths between moments I was buried in the ground.

Then it was absolute agony.

I felt him grab below my wrist, and before I knew what was happening, he thrust a long, thick metal spike through my hand. I screamed bloody murder as he took a mallet from his burlap sack and hammered the big piece of metal deeper into the ground beneath my hand. I barely had time to think about it before I felt him grab my other hand.

"No, no please!" I screamed, knowing the pain that was about to come. The second one hurt even worse. I felt every inch of it as he hammered the steel through my flesh. Ripping, tearing, burning sensations swept through my body. This pain, it was unlike anything I'd ever felt before. All I could do was scream and thrash and beg. "Stop it! Please, stop!" I cried. "Why are you doing this to me?"

The Bull Man offered only a grunt in response before finally lifting his weight off my back and shuffling back over to the canvas spread. I looked up at him through teary eyes, watching him reload his sack and go. I tasted blood on my lip. My head and my whole body hurt, laying there on my belly, arms fully spread as I was crucified to the ground.

And as if nothing had happened, that son-of-a-bitch disappeared into the darkness.

12

I was there for what felt like eternity. Everything hurt so bad. At first all I could do was cry. Who could do something like this to someone? Why me? I just wanted my dad. I wanted to see Ginny, my friends, anything but the Bull Man and this torture chamber. While I lay there, viciously spiked and hopelessly alone, I kept seeing scenes from my childhood, like the time my dad took Ginny and I to the state fair when we were just girls. I was nine and Ginny was eight, and we were so excited to go. We waited all year for the fall festival. We had hot dogs, candy apples, and fried dough, and we spent the day just wandering around, looking at animals, talking to people, and having fun with my dad. It was easy to take that stuff for granted. I think the reason I thought about this, other than my life flashing before me in my state of near-death, was because of the Ferris wheel. I was so damn scared of that thing. Every year, my dad tried to make me go on it, and I always said no. He'd always push me and say, "Come on, it's not so bad, I promise. You can see the whole countryside." I'd start crying and shaking my head, falling to the ground and going dead weight if I had to in order to escape his grip. No way I was going on that thing. But when I was nine, I finally got on it. I don't even remember how he convinced me, but the second we started moving up I was screaming and crying. Every second I thought I was going to die. Worse, I couldn't do anything about it because we were trapped in that seat, ascending the great wheel of doom. It was the scariest ten minutes of my life waiting to get back around to the bottom. I was traumatized for years after that. In my dungeon, staked to the ground and fighting for my life, I kind of felt like that, though obviously my current situation was more dire. I could really die, I kept thinking. Sure, I could've died on the Ferris wheel too, but now ... this was real. This wasn't chance. I had to fight, or I was going to die.

... But what could I do?

I mean, there was no way out of this, was there?

I had nearly given in to this notion, but as I examined my limited view of the darkness in front of me I noticed a glint, an anomaly of texture in the blackness. A copper key.

Hope.

After a moment of considering this, I decided: no more self-pitying. It was time I started sucking it up and assessing my situation. I reminded myself of what I had thought in the beginning, when I had first woken up in this place. The women who survived these things always overcame long odds. There was always a way; the question was did I have the will to find it? *Goddamn right*

I did. No matter how bad the pain was, it wasn't the point. I needed to soldier up and figure it out. I pictured my dad standing beside me, telling me not to give up, telling me I was going to live if I just pushed myself a little harder. I was no quitter.

I stopped crying and started to really focus on what I was going to have to do. That key I had endured such violence to earn was in front of me, just waiting to set me free, but before I could worry about that, I had to get my hands free. There was only one way I could think of to do that. Taking a deep breath, I pressed my chest into the dirt to brace myself and lifted my hands as aggressively as I could.

"Oh fuck!" I cried in agony as the stakes rebuked my attempt to escape by tearing new bits of flesh. They barely budged. I realized the problem was, these things were over a foot long and buried deep in this hard, rocky soil. Plus, there were studs at the top of each one, so there was no way I could pull my hands off the spikes from the exposed end. I was going to have to get the spikes up out of the ground first, then out of my hands. I tried again and again to lift my hands, but I was truly stuck. Changing strategies, I tried getting my knees up under me, but no matter how I shifted my body I just couldn't do it with my arms stretched out as they were. Frustrated, I kicked my feet around in the dirt, screeching, "Fuck you!" into the darkness before collapsing back into tears.

A moment later, I kicked my feet again out of frustration, and in my tantrum, I felt my foot kick the stone wall beside me. Curious, I shifted my body that way and put my foot out again. I was pretty close to the wall. I could feel the grooves and the uneven bumps along it, and after a minute, I found a part that jutted out a couple inches, just enough that I thought I could use it as leverage.

I got my left foot up first, the one closer the wall, then pressed my foot into the groove hard enough to support my weight as I lifted my torso up and crossed my right foot under my left leg and pressed it down on top of my left foot as hard as I could. Putting all my weight on my right wrist, I pushed off the wall with my feet and tried to lift my left hand. Gritting my teeth, I fought through the pain, twisting my torso and pushing off the wall as hard as I could. I could feel it moving. The stake was coming out of the ground, inch by agonizing inch, the metal scraping around inside my hand with every tug, blood squirting out and dripping into the dirt. It was the absolute worst pain I had felt in my life, but it was working. I had to stop a couple times and recoup, but after a few more good thrusts off the wall I had the stake high enough out of the dirt that I could curl my left knee up to my chest. It got easier then, when I could power upward, and before long, I freed my left hand from the ground. The spike was still in it, but at least I could sit up.

After a short break I went back to work, standing straight up and tugging the right stake up from the ground. With my hands finally unearthed, I wasted no time pulling the long metal spikes out of my palms. Blood began spilling all over me as I unplugged the holes. Luckily, the spikes were long, not super thick, so I thought I was going to be ok as long as I wrapped them. Working quickly, I packed the wounds with dirt, stopping the bleeding for the most part. Next, I started pulling my shirt off, thinking the long sleeves would work perfectly as bandages if I tore them off. Unfortunately, I realized I couldn't do that because the shackles were still stopping me. *Wait! The key!* Desperately, I scrambled on hands and knees around the blood-soaked dirt, searching for the precious copper lifeline. Every second, I was reminded of the terrible agony of my wounds. I couldn't put pressure on my hands. Instead, I had to shift around on my knees while running my fingers along the soil and rock until I felt it, that wonderful, lifesaving copper. Holding it in my hands, I fumbled about, dropping it once before getting a firm grip and bringing it close enough to my face to see. It was still there, thank you, God. The key was there. But would it open the shackles?

I prayed so hard while I jerked my wrists around and found the keyhole. In it went, and with surprising ease, my left shackle was off. *Oh my God!* I took off the right one, and practically did a backflip I was so relieved. I was free! I would see Ginny and my dad again!

All I had to do now was get out of this place.

I went back to the task of nursing my hands. Taking off my Henley, I used one of the spikes to tear the sleeves, then ripped them off and wrapped the fabric tightly around each of my hands.

When I finally finished, and my adrenaline began to wear off, I collapsed with my back to the wall, closing my eyes and resting my head on the stone.

An overwhelming exhaustion came over me—a combination of early dehydration, stress, fear, and just about everything else.

What was I doing there? Who did this to me?

I knew what came next. I had to go into the dark. I knew I had to make a plan, but my head was pounding as bad as anything. I'd had migraines before, but this was worse. It wasn't just my head either; it was like a full body migraine, a persistent, strength-sapping state indescribable by any normal human sensibilities. Well, I hadn't eaten, I remembered. I had this water, but it wasn't enough, not for how much stress my body was under. Add lack of sleep and brutal mutilation ... yeah, it was safe to say I was running on fumes. All the more reason I needed to get out of there as soon as possible. My brain was telling me this, yet my body wasn't responding. It was all too much. I started to cry again.

Why did Jake get the key, but I didn't? That had been bothering me the whole time I was lying there on those spikes. Why did the Bull Man punish me for taking the key?

Nothing made sense, but my head was hurting worse trying to think about it. I couldn't stay here anymore! It was time to go.

13

I took the time to inventory myself before I set off. I took one of the spikes to use as a weapon if I encountered the Bull Man on my way through the tunnels; to take both spikes would have been cumbersome and unrealistic. I needed a free hand to feel around. I checked my hands and made sure the bandages were tightened as much as I could get them, and I rolled up my pant legs. I don't know why I did this, but it made me feel like I could move better. Unfortunately, I was still barefoot, but I would just have to deal with it. I decided the water bottle would hamper me as well, and possibly make noise, so I drank the rest and left the plastic bottle in my corner. Finally, I slid the copper key into my pocket and began my journey. The darkness seemed to change as I ventured away from my humble chain block. It was as if it was angry that I was encroaching upon it, like it was closing in around me, narrowing its eyes, and preparing to strike.

God, I was so scared, so anxious to get out, but I took it slow anyway. *Be careful for traps*, I kept repeating in my head. Also, I wondered how long before the Bull Man was coming down my tunnel again? It couldn't be long. That scared me too, because what if he came down while I was escaping? I couldn't think about it.

I was clutching the spike in my right hand and dragging my left hand along the stone wall to guide myself, and after about two or three minutes, my hand slid off the wall. A junction? To be sure, I stepped to my right and reached out to feel the wall. It was still solid on that side, but what about ahead? I stepped back to the left until I felt the corner again, then stepped straight forward until my hand crashed into another corner. Ok, it's a T-junction.

Left or straight?

Left or straight?

Which way was the way out, and which one would kill me?

If I chose wrong, I wondered if I would be able to get back. I needed to mark this junction somehow, and mark which direction I came from.

Then, I heard the roar. The murderous scream that meant the Bull Man was coming down the tunnel any second. My heart about stopped. Which direction would he come from? No time to think! Oh God! He was going to kill me! What was I supposed to do?

It came to me abruptly: the footsteps! *Fight the fear, listen for the footsteps.*

The familiar scuffing sounds, rocks kicking up, dirt kicking, all seemed to be coming from straight ahead. It was hard to be a hundred percent sure of the direction, but it was getting closer and there was no more time to deliberate.

I made my decision.

Left.

I hadn't taken ten steps down the tunnel when I felt a wind at my back as the Bull Man rushed straight through where I had just been standing. I heard his footsteps clear as crystal. Right behind me. I could even hear his labored breathing and his snorting noises as he shuffled by. I had to press myself against the wall and hold my breath for fear of giving myself away.

Thank God.

He was moving away, down the tunnel toward my chain block. I breathed a huge sigh of relief.

But wait! My eyes went wide and my heart skipped a beat. He would find my chain block empty, and when he did he'd know I went this way. It was the only other way to go.

I had to find somewhere to hide, and I had to do it fast.

14

Panic shot through my limbs, propelling me forward like my feet were rockets. There would be another junction to my left, and not far from here, I suspected. Jake's tunnel was right next to mine, so it had to be here. Hastily, I used my left hand to drag my fingers across the bumpy stone, searching for the opening. When at last I found it, I heard the Bull Man roar in the distance. A new wave of fear swept over me as I dove into Jake's tunnel.

I slowed myself to a power walk once I got into the tunnel, making sure that if the tunnel curved, I wouldn't go crashing into the wall. Somehow, in that moment of desperation, I had the presence of mind to realize that I had gone far enough in the previous tunnel that this one must bend left somewhere, because Jake had literally been right behind my wall.

I'd only gone in a few feet when another problem occurred to me: the Bull Man might come there next. He had obviously found me missing. The question was, would he come looking for me, or ignore it, like he seemed to do when Jake escaped? Then again, I didn't know if he ignored it. I had been so busy escaping the spikes, I had lost track of how much time had passed. For all I knew, this was not a normal rotation. The Bull Man might have gone after Jake. He may even have found him. After all, where was Jake? I hadn't so much as heard a whimper of him since he ventured away from his chain block.

I couldn't risk it. If this tunnel was a dead end like the one I'd been chained up in, I was dead. So, I spun around and went back to the junction, where I decided to go left, away from my original tunnel. I could hear the Bull Man coming back up my tunnel now. My heart was pounding out of my chest. I had no idea where this new tunnel would go, but weighing the odds, I thought my chances were better with this one than Jake's tunnel.

I had no idea how far I went. It seemed really far, but I had to keep going because I heard him behind me. It seemed like he slowed down, but I sure didn't. A good way in, I stubbed my toe on a rock and fell right on my face. I heard the spike clang on the rock as I fell. Covering my mouth and squinting my eyes, I tried not to cry out, though my toe was in total agony. I felt it and there was definitely blood, and my toenail felt cracked.

I heard the Bull Man grunting, having perhaps heard me.

Hustling to my feet, I limped along for a second before adapting to the pain and picking up the pace. At last I felt the wall give way to another junction, and without hesitation I dove down the tunnel to my left and continued feeling my way on. I listened carefully as I progressed, trying to gauge whether the Bull Man had come the same way as me. Thankfully, he seemed to have moved away. When I couldn't hear him at all anymore, I stopped momentarily and sat down, wincing as I accidently leaned too far on my cracked toe. Careful not to make any noise, I used the sharp end of the spike to poke a couple holes in my shirt, near the bottom, then put my fingers into the hole and slowly tore at them, until I had a little strip of fabric to wrap my toe. It was painstaking this way, but I didn't know how close the Bull Man was and I couldn't afford to tear the shirt like I had before and risk making noise. When I was done patching myself up, I let my head fall back onto the wall and closed my eyes for a moment. My hands hurt so bad, and now my toe. For a brief moment, I had to collect myself.

Ok, Lani. You got this, girl. Forget about the pain. You are out of the chains, now what comes next?

Oh, shit!

I hadn't marked the way I came! I had been in such a panic when I heard the Bull Man coming ... oh no. I know I went left out of my tunnel, then left again after Jake's tunnel. Ok, that was easy. I was in a third tunnel. There was mine, then Jake's, and then the one I was currently in. The Bull Man had been behind me, and he wasn't now, which meant he either turned back or there was another junction along the way I had just come from. I wondered if the tunnel I was in at the moment would be a dead end as well, like mine and Jake's. If so, I figured I had better get out of there soon. This time, I needed to mark where I was going. Maybe I could use the rocks on the ground to make arrows, or use the spike to dig them—

Wait a second. Something felt off. My head wasn't being jabbed by the uneven walls. In fact, it felt constructed, splintered, almost like ... wood!

Excitedly, I turned around, sitting on my knees, and felt along the wall, until my hand bumped into a little round knob.

I had found a door.

15

"Hello?" A woman's voice pierced the dark as I edged the door halfway open. On the other side of the door I couldn't see anything. It was as dark and hopeless as the rest of the tunnels. I froze. For a second I didn't know what to make of what I was hearing. My default reaction was to assume everything in this place was against me, but then I recalled that Jake had begun this hellish trial chained up just like me. The woman called again, "Hello? Is someone there? Please, no more. I promise, I won't try to escape again."

"Hey," I whispered back, "Don't worry, I'm not him."

"Huh?" She sounded panicked. "Who are you?" She was thinking the same thing as me; that if someone had come for her it must mean they were here to get her.

"Be quiet, he'll hear! It's ok, I woke up trapped here, too. Don't worry, I'm gonna get you out."

I had it in my mind, for some reason, that my copper key was going to work on her chains as well. Not sure why. It seemed a little unlikely, really thinking about it. But either way, I wasn't about to leave her.

I let the door swing the rest of the way open and took two steps into the room.

"Stop!" she exclaimed.

"Shhhh! It's ok," I tried to calm her. He was going to hear us. My heart started pounding again at the thought.

"There's a trap in the middle of the room."

"What?"

Squinting my eyes, I could make out a trace of a woman's silhouette straight ahead. She seemed to be standing upright, her arms held out, and her legs spread apart.

She leaned toward me, and I heard the familiar rattle of chains as her weight fell on them. "Hug the wall. There's a beartrap somewhere in the middle. I heard him set it."

My God, who the hell was this guy? He was seriously deranged.

"Ok, hold on, I'm coming."

"Be careful."

That's exactly what I did. I used the spike like a blind man's cane, guiding my step as I shuffled along the right wall.

When I reached the back of the room, she said, "In that corner somewhere, there's a lighter."

"He offered you the items, too? Who the hell is this guy?"

"I don't know, but can you please hurry? He'll be back soon."

I fell to my knees and started searching around for the lighter. It didn't take me long to find it, and along with the lighter, I also found some of the Bull Man's bread. Without a thought, I took a big bite of the precious resource, closing my eyes and savoring every morsel.

"Hello?" the woman pushed. "Did you find it?"

"Got it," I said, swallowing my bread with instant guilt. I saved the rest of it for her and hurried over to help her. God only knew what she went through to get that bread. Standing right in front of her, I flicked on the lighter, and the dim, orange glow revealed a whole other level of horror to me.

"Cadence?!" I almost yelled. Before me was my best friend since grade school, her wrists shackled to the wall and her shirtless torso covered in burns and cuts. Her face was a mess, devastated by bruises and streaked with dried up tears and blood.

"Cadence! Oh my God, what did he do to you?"

No wonder she hadn't been answering my or Ginny's texts. This poor girl must have been down here for at least three days. And we didn't even come looking for her. What kind of friends were we?

"Lani?" She sobbed. "Oh no, no, no, no. He got you too."

"Cadence, it's ok, I'm gonna get you out of here, you understand?"

As I leaned in toward her face and tried to touch

Bottom of the Well

her, Cadence stiffened her whole body and said sharply, "Don't!"

I stopped for a second and stared at her. I saw her eyes shift down and to the left, and that's when I looked down as well and noticed why she was so stiff. Between her lower back and the wall were about a dozen metal spikes jutting out from the wall and pressing their sharp tips against her skin. The way she was standing, she had to arch her back to avoid the spikes pressing into her. This was so messed up. I had to get us out of here.

"Ok, I see." I addressed the spikes as calmly as I could, trying to keep her from freaking out. "Don't worry, I'm gonna get you down."

Fetching the copper key from my pocket, I held the lighter up to one of Cadence's wrists and got a good grip on the shackle. I placed my thumb over the keyhole, so I'd be able to find it in the dark, and flipped the lighter closed to conserve fuel. As I started finicking with the lock, Cadence asked, "Lani, why is he doing this to us?"

"I don't know."

Talking over me, she continued, "I want to go home. I want to see my mom and my sister. I don't want to die ..."

"Shhh!" I warned as her voice began to rise.

"I just want to go. Just want to go."

"I know. And we going to escape. I promise."

Of course, my key didn't seem to be working as

well as I thought it would, and honestly, if it didn't, I had no idea how I was going to free her.

The chains attaching Cadence to the wall clanged repeatedly as my fingers fumbled around the keyhole in her shackle. My hands weren't working right, being in crazy pain and being wrapped in my shirt. After missing the keyhole a couple times, I got it to line up, but when I tried to push it in, my fingers slipped off the key and it fell to the dirt.

"Sorry, hold on, Cadence. I'm getting you out," I apologized.

As I bent down to search for the key, I heard the distant moan of the Bull Man. Cadence shrieked, her wrists flinching as her body tensed and the chains began rattling anew.

"Lani, you have to hurry. He is coming!"

"I know, I know. Hold still."

I found the key and was working on the lock again while Cadence did her best to hold herself steady through labored, anxious breaths. We heard the Bull Man again, closer this time. Close enough I could start to hear his movements. Shit, the key was not going to work, I realized. If I waited any longer, the Bull Man would arrive, and if he saw the door open he'd know I was there. Neither of us would escape if I let him catch me now. Cadence was going to hate me, but I had to leave her for the time being.

I did my best to break the news to her. "Cadence, this key doesn't fit, I'm sorry."

"Try the other side, maybe ..."

"No, it's the wrong key. I'm so, so sorry. I have to leave."

"What, no!"

"Shhh! He's coming. I promise, I'll come back for you, but if he finds me in here, we are both dead."

"No, Lani, please don't leave me with him."

My heart hurt so bad listening to the desperation in her voice. I imagined myself in her position, chained up on those spikes, the Bull Man on his way to deliver fresh punishment. I'd be crying too. I'd be begging for my dad and my sister, and I'd be screaming at Cadence, asking her how she could even consider leaving me. But I wasn't the one on the spikes. I had escaped from mine, and I knew that had happened for a reason. The reason was, I had to get us out. If I got caught now, it was all for nothing. This was my responsibility to make this decision, and to figure out how to save us.

"I'm so sorry. I promise, I'll come back."

"No, no, no. Please, Lani, no."

I made my way back around the perimeter of the room, listening to Cadence's terrified cries. Although she continued sobbing and begging the Bull Man to let her go, she understood enough not to call out to me after I was away from her and give me away to him. When I got into the outside tunnel, I closed the door carefully behind me and ventured further down the tunnel, away from the intersection where the Bull Man would come from. A short distance from the door, I was able to duck around a corner into a connecting tunnel, where I pressed my back to the wall and listened. The door swung open, and the Bull Man grunted before going inside. All the while, I heard Cadence pleading with him to give her mercy, not to hurt her anymore. I couldn't bear the thought of abandoning her and letting whatever was about to happen befall her. I just had to get us out of there. But how? I could feel myself beginning to get frantic, urgent for action, but I knew I had to be more calculated. Both our lives depended on it. I turned in place for a moment, finding myself wanting to pace, but fearful of making noise. My arms swung at my sides while I thought. I wanted to sit for a second, to think through my next action, but I was too hyped up. I had to do something! Then, my hand brushed past my jeans, and I felt the piece of paper in my pocket crinkle. And then, I had an idea.

    I could draw a map!

16

I had plenty of room on the paper, and I had a light source. The only thing was, how would I write it? Mud, maybe? No, it would smudge and possibly ruin the paper, and I wouldn't have seen it clearly anyway. What else did I have? I looked at my bandaged hands. *Ok, there's an idea.*

Carefully, I unwrapped my left hand. With the right, I gently poked into my wound with the spike, just enough to open a little of it with fresh blood, and I coated my right index finger. Then I flicked on the lighter with my left hand and held it beside the paper, which I had unfolded on the ground in front of me.

This could work.

Pressing my finger carefully to the paper, I began marking what I knew about the tunnels so far with my crimson ink. I started with three landmarks: my chain block, Jake's block, and Cadence's chamber. *Let's see ...* When I escaped my chains, I took a left out of my tunnel. I knew Jake's tunnel was next to mine, so I could fill that in. After Jake's tunnel, there was a four-way intersection—the one I had just passed through before finding Cadence. Currently I was at the end of Cadence's tunnel, and I had turned right. If there was a way out, I guessed it would be wherever the Bull Man was coming from, which would be somewhere on the other side of the intersection. So far, all three of us were held captive on the same side, which for now I was calling the "south" side of the main, horizontal tunnel. I had yet to go into any part of the "north" side, but I knew that at least my original tunnel and the tunnel north of the four-way intersection went that way. The Bull Man seemed to come from my tunnel, so that was probably my best bet. If I went right then, while he was with Cadence, I could possibly beat him back there.

Wait a second.

Where was Jake?

It just occurred to me, as I saw the "J" I had marked to represent Jake's chain block, that I hadn't heard him at all. I'd gone through a few tunnels since I left. Was the maze really that big? Or was Jake dead? Or maybe there was another explanation. I flipped over the paper to the side where the Bull Man had written his clue. "I'm closer than you think."

Jake could be the Bull Man.

He was tall enough, and actually, everything that had happened so far sort of aligned with this theory. Well, no. I realized that Jake had been hollering when the Bull Man was in my tunnel, so it couldn't be him. That made no sense. But I supposed he could be working with the Bull Man. I didn't know why he would be, but somehow, I just felt it was a possibility. I mean, why else would the Bull Man have let Jake go free without a punishment? Look what he did to me and Cadence.

I heard a shrill, tortured scream from Cadence's chamber and snapped out of my deliberation. There was no time to consider this now. Cadence was suffering and I had to make a decision. I looked at the map again. *If I go right now, I can make it.* Before I could let my nerves get the better of me, I folded up the paper and hurried back though the tunnels.

17

It was about a week before the party at Cole's house when Ginny and I had been at Cadence's house hanging out. That was the last time I'd seen her, besides a couple times in class. We were supposed to be studying for midterms, but we were doing a much better job of procrastinating. Ginny and Cadence sat cross-legged on the soft white area rug in the middle of Cadence's room, books open in front of them, and I was stretched across Cadence's bed with my stuff laid out beside me.

"Seriously, like, how am I gonna remember this stuff?" Ginny complained.

"You will," Cadence reassured her. "We still have time. Don't stress, girl."

"I feel like I could look at this stuff for years and not be able to write a paper on it."

I gave Ginny my two cents: "Just remember, you don't have to get an A. C's get degrees."

Ginny laughed. "True talk. I don't want a C, though. This class is seriously the only one I struggle with. Like, why is it so hard?"

"Well, Professor Keaton is not exactly a peach," I said. It definitely wasn't Ginny's fault. I mean, yeah, she could pay attention more in class, but all of us could. I knew she took notes, at least. It's just that anthropology is a hard subject, and Keaton is one tough asshole.

"Yeah, seriously. I mean, when am I ever gonna need to know this shit again?" Ginny asked.

"I don't know," Cadence said. "Should we make index cards?"

Ginny had pulled out her phone and started scrolling, so I imagined she had no intention of doing that. I was pretty spent myself, and unlike Ginny, I didn't care if I got a C. Not in anthropology anyway. I was going to be a lacrosse coach and a personal trainer. I wanted to coach at the college level, but I'd have to coach high school first, most likely. I wasn't sure. All I knew was, I was athletic, driven, and really good at training. My coaches told me I had an affinity for driving people to do their best, both because of my positive attitude and no excuses approach. And between playing sports and volunteering, I had tons of connections around Pennsylvania. I'd made state three times in high school, once with the lacrosse team and twice in track and field. I even had the school record for shotput in tenth grade. So even if I didn't get to coach a college team right away, I could definitely get my foot in the door somewhere.

That got me thinking about lacrosse, and I pulled out my phone and started looking at my training schedule for the week. I opened a new email from the assistant coach and was in the middle of reading it when Ginny shoved her phone toward me.

Excitedly, she said, "Yo, check this guy Tiago out! He's liking all my shit. He's pretty hot, right?"

I thought he was kind of a fake when I saw his profile pictures. I mean, he was hot, and it wasn't, like, terrible. I guess he wasn't that fake; he just had a couple stupid pictures, like ones with him shirtless holding beers. My dad always taught me not to take pictures like that if I wanted to be an athlete. Well, he would have rather I not drink at all. But that wasn't realistic, and he probably knew that, so posting clean photos would have to suffice.

"Wow, get it, girl," I said as I did a quick scroll through Ginny's posts and noted all the thumbs ups from her new admirer.

"We met the other day at the café. He requested me, like, an hour later."

"You're not going on with that Cole guy?" Cadence asked.

Ginny scoffed. "Cole? Nah, he's cool, but not my type."

"Really? Well, you seem like his type," I commented.

"Yeah, he keeps inviting me places. I go whenever there's a group, 'cause whatever, but I'm not trying to go on any moonlit walks on the beach with him."

Ginny was typing like a madwoman on her phone,

and at this point, Cadence was engrossed in something on hers as well. I had lost interest in the email I had started reading, which turned out to be just a generic weekly update thing, and I fell back onto Cadence's pillow and closed my eyes for a second.

"I guess Cole's throwing a party next weekend," Cadence said. "I bet he'll invite you."

Ginny laughed. "Listen, if there's free booze, I'll go. Like I said, ain't no romance happening, but a house party? Hell yeah."

I let my head drift to the right, and when I opened my eyes, I was looking down at the street through Cadence's window. She had one of those cheesy, old-school window-seat things, with the white latticed windowpanes and the wooden platform under it. She had it lined with all her childhood stuffed animals, which I always thought was super cute. I grabbed her stuffed lion and squeezed it close to my chest, rubbing my chin on its fluffy mane. I got rid of all my stuffies when I got to high school because I was embarrassed of them, but I kind of regretted that now. That little lion was so comforting. It almost made me cry, thinking about my little white Coca-Cola polar bear suffocating under piles of landfill garbage somewhere. Sometimes I wished I were still a kid.

Then I looked back out the window and saw something weird. There was a guy in a raincoat and a fisherman's hat standing in the middle of the sidewalk.

That's right! I *had* seen that guy before! My apartment wasn't the first time. I had seen this asshole that night at Cadence's parent's house. I didn't think much of it that night, though. I remember thinking it was weird, that he was standing there, but I had pushed it out of my mind. I'd told myself that maybe he was waiting for someone, and I decided that if he was still there after a little bit I would say something. But a minute later, he was gone. I wish I'd said something, because now that I realized there was a connection between the two nights, I may have had someone else to validate it.

But it wouldn't matter if I died in these tunnels.

I quickened my pace back to my original tunnel, and when I reached the junction I moved hastily up the way the Bull Man had come. I still didn't hear any sign of him behind me, so that was good, I supposed. Although I couldn't think about what that meant for Cadence.

There was another connection from the previous days, before I woke up in this hellhole, I realized randomly as I felt my way along the tunnel. The night Sami and I were at my place, we went outside after, because I was too freaked out to be in that house after seeing that man outside my bedroom. The cops showed up and we were sitting there on the stoop. I was crying and Sami had his arms around me, stroking my hair and just doing his best to comfort me. He'd gone back upstairs to get me some clothes so I wouldn't be half naked out in my yard, and he'd stood guard while I got dressed just inside the front entrance of my apartment.

There had been two cops; one was sort of rough, a seasoned looking guy, tall and lanky, with a full mustache and scraggly, unkempt facial hair, and the other was a built, stern-looking blonde woman. The man said something as he was getting out of the car and began casing the yard immediately, his flashlight scanning the bushes beside the house.

The woman approached me and asked, "Ma'am, are you all right?"

"Yeah," I said, still too much in shock to articulate further.

"You said there was a man in your house. Did he come in the front door?"

Sami answered for me. "The front door was left open, so yeah, I'm guessing that's how he came in."

"Do you keep the door locked at night?" the policewoman asked.

"Yes, I always lock it," I replied with disgust. What kind of question was that? I was a college-age girl living in the suburbs, and my roommate was never home, so I was basically alone. Obviously I locked my door.

"Ok, ok. Did you see where the man went?"

Sami answered again. "By the time we got downstairs, he was gone. I never even saw him, but Lani did."

"Wait, you never saw the man?" she asked. "Lani, right? Do you remember what he looked like?"

I had to think about it for a minute, mostly because I was just out of it, not because I didn't remember. I remembered all too well. That was the scariest shit of my life. I told her what I'd seen, minus the fact that I was certain I had seen him standing where he couldn't be standing. I was already worried these people were going to think I was nuts without any ghost stories added to the mix.

I'm glad I left that out, too. Looking back now, I know it wasn't a ghost, because now I recognized I'd seen him at Cadence's house as well. Plus, there was this other connection between the two nights ...

After I was done describing the guy to the officer, she had turned back to the street for a second, then back to me, and asked, "Whose green station wagon is that?"

It hadn't been mine, and it definitely wasn't Sami's Camaro. Plus, there was no way it was there when we got home, because where the wagon was parked was where I'd tripped and Sami caught me and helped me over the curb. Also, I was positive that this same car had been sitting on the curb outside Cadence's house that night a week before. I could see it so clearly in my mind. I just knew I wasn't imagining it.

The note ... "I'm closer than you think." Was it him? Raincoat guy, was he the Bull Man? But what about

Jake? Was it really possible Jake was involved somehow? Technically, Jake could have followed me after the party. Damn it, I just didn't know.

Suddenly, I felt my leg slip, and my whole body slid down into the dirt. Panicking, I clawed at the wall and kicked my other foot under me. I managed to land on solid ground, one ankle under me and the other dangling over the edge of some unknown abyss. My heart was absolutely racing.

When I gathered myself, I flicked on the lighter and realized that there was a drop-off in front of me. I couldn't tell how far across this pit was, nor precisely how deep, but from the faint orange glimmer of the flame I could just make out the shape of several sharp wooden spikes below. *Oh my God.* That would be the worst way to go. It would take so long to die if I landed the wrong way.

Ok, so did I have to turn around?

No, there had to be a way over to the other side. This was where the Bull Man came from, so it couldn't be just a pit. Maybe there was a door on the other wall that I hadn't been following. Holding the light off to the right of where I was sitting, I scanned the area and noticed a small, narrow path that jutted forward across the ditch.

Oh, hell no.

I crawled closer to examine my finding, and sure enough, it was a land bridge, flanked on either side by spike pits. As much as I hated it, I knew this had to be the way to go. There were no doors are any other discernable path nearby. So, I took a few seconds to compose myself, took a deep breath, and began to cross the narrow pass.

One foot in front of the other, I told myself, making sure to press my foot down lightly before putting my weight on the ground each time I went forward. For all I knew, there would be collapsing rocks in the middle of this thing. Everything else in this maze seemed to be rigged.

I'd taken quite a few steps across the bridge before I stopped cold, my feet planted firmly mere inches from the death below. Cold sweat rushed into me like the surge before a storm. I don't know how close I was to the other side at the time, but I guess it was close enough, because in that moment I suddenly had this weird feeling. I'd felt it before, and I knew exactly what it meant. I just knew the Bull Man was standing right there on the other side waiting for me.

18

When I was a little girl, I was distinctly afraid of my grandparent's upstairs bedroom. It wasn't the one I slept in; that room was fine. Rather, it was the adjacent bedroom that bothered me. Whenever I slept up there alone, I always got really anxious. My hair would stand on end and I'd start getting goosebumps. I'd always feel like someone was watching me. I don't know why, because I never saw anything in that house, but I could never quite shake the feeling. Sometimes I'd lie there and just stare into the hallway, determined that if something was coming for me, I was going to see it coming first and get the hell out of dodge. Most of the time, I got scared after thirty seconds or so of gazing into the darkness and hid under my blanket. My grandma never understood it, but I swear to God there was something in that other bedroom, and it was always watching me from across the hall.

That's exactly how I felt as I stood stiff as a board in the middle of the narrow bridge, stuck between fear and indecision.

A few seconds passed. I knew he was there. My mind was frantic, searching for alternatives I knew weren't there. Finally, I turned around and made a run for it.

The Bull Man roared and came after me at a

startling speed. Once we cleared the bridge, I heard his feet stomping in the dirt at a tempo I had yet to encounter. This wasn't his standard rush—he was coming to kill me this time.

I ran as fast as my poor bare feet could go, almost buckling twice when my arches landed on pebbles in the dirt. All it was going to take was one good sharp one and I was on my face. Then, I'd be dead. *I should have taken the shoes instead of the water.*

He roared again as he closed in on me and I felt frantically along the wall for the intersection. *Please, please*, I prayed.

Where is it?

I could almost feel the Bull Man's breath on me, he was so close. He started taunting me, scraping his axe along the stones in the wall as he chased me. He could catch me any time, I realized. This psycho was just messing with me. I was so scared there were no words for it.

Finally, my hand slipped off the stone and I stumbled forward into the other tunnel. My knees hit the dirt for a second, and in my desperate shuffle, I dropped the spike. Part of me thought I should reach for it, but instead, I left it and hurried to my feet, bolting down the tunnel. I rushed recklessly down the dark path until I found another opening and dodged into it. I wasn't sure I knew this tunnel, but really, I had nowhere else to go. The axe was still following me, grinding away, and I knew I had to think of something fast. I couldn't outrun him, and at this point, I couldn't hide either. I'd lost the spike, so I had no way to fight. What the hell was I supposed to do? For the first time since the very beginning of the ordeal, I was almost certain I wasn't getting out of there alive.

I heard him growl, hot on my tail, and I couldn't hold back my tears as I became overwhelmed with fear. "No, no, please, let me go!"

Just when I thought it couldn't get worse, I ran headlong into a wall. *Oh no! Please don't be a dead end!*

Feeling around wildly, desperately, my hand found a wall to my right, then my left. The corners were closing me in. My heart sank into my stomach. That was it; I was dead. I don't know what I thought I could do, but I started clawing at the wall, crying and begging the Bull Man, "Please! Please don't kill me! I'll do anything!"

I felt his presence over me, and suddenly, my hand slipped into the wall, and I fell forward against what seemed to be a large crack in the stone. Full of adrenaline and survival instinct, I straightened out my body and crawled inside the crevice as fast as I could. As I pulled my feet inside, the Bull Man's axe came crashing down in the dirt where I had just been crouched. With incredible rage, he lifted the axe and smashed it several times at the wall where the crack was, chipping away at the stone as he did. The crevice seemed to go deeper, so I continued to crawl back away from the axe-wielding maniac. Eventually, he gave up and I heard him bellow in his normal fashion before stomping away, back into the maze.

19

Trapped. Hopeless. Powerless. Defeated.

Those were among my emotions, as faintly as I could articulate them at that moment, while plastered between two walls in that thin, harrowing space. The Bull Man was gone now. It sounded like he had been headed back toward mine and Jake's original tunnels, but I was so disoriented, I wasn't certain of my position. So, really, he could have been going anywhere.

Feeling myself start to panic, I managed to stand up in the narrow space and rip the little piece of paper and the lighter out of my pockets. My shaky hands unfolded the paper and pressed it against the wall. I lit the lighter and held it up toward the map to try and make sense of where I was. That passage was so tight that I had to hold the lighter off to the side because I was afraid of burning the paper, so I really couldn't see the map well. It was ok, I could see it just enough, and I had it memorized anyway. I just needed an anchor point so I could figure out where I went from the bridge until now.

Then I heard a whisper.

"Lani. Psst, Lani."

Gripped with terror, I killed the light and jammed

the lighter back in my pocket. I started folding the map and looking around me.

"Lani, over here," the voice called again.

Wait, I knew that voice!

"Jake?" I replied.

"Yeah, it's me. To your right."

My head snapped toward him, and I could see a small flicker of fire deep in the crack. Jake's silhouette was dimly visible behind the flame.

"Jake! Oh my God, you're alive!"

"Shh! Come on, I found a way out."

"What?" On the outside, I whispered in disbelief, but on the inside, I was screaming. Hallelujah, there was a God. Jake had found the way out, and he must have been coming back to get me. I almost didn't want to believe it, just in case. I wasn't sure my heart could take it.

"Shh!" he reiterated. "Come on."

Wasting no more time, I began carefully moving through the crevice, feeling along one side with my back to the other.

Urgently, Jake added, "Be careful. There are razorblades." I stopped cold. *Of course there are.* "Use your light," he instructed.

Doing as he said, I held my arm out in front of me and flicked the lighter on. I looked up and down the walls in front of me and it seemed safe, so I pressed on. A few steps in, I saw what he was talking about. Embedded into the wall, at about the level where I would place my hand, was a two-inch razor blade. On further inspection of the area I found another on the opposite wall, a foot or so ahead of the first one. That would have torn into my back if Jake hadn't told me. What about the ground? If I got one in my foot, that was the end. I scanned carefully and the coast seemed to be clear, so I timidly navigated around the blades in the wall. I did this the entire way, and toward the end I could tell the lighter was almost out of fluid, because I had to keep reigniting it. I hadn't thought of that until now, but it was very possible I was going to be totally in the dark soon. Good thing Jake still had his. I put mine out as I reached the end of the crevice and let Jake's light guide me the rest of the way.

"Ok, there you go," Jake said, grabbing my arm and helping me out the other end of the passageway. He put his light out and wrapped his arms around me. Surprised, I jumped at first, but quickly realized what was happening and gladly accepted his embrace. "Lani, I'm so glad you are ok," he said.

Wrapping my arms around him and sobbing into his shoulder, I replied, "Me, too. I thought you were dead."

"I'm sorry I left you."

That made me think about Cadence, and I got a lump in my throat. She was still back there, probably, suffering on those spikes, and I had no way of helping her. The thought of it just made me that much more desperate to escape and get help.

"No, I understand," I said to him as we released each other. "I found my friend Cadence in one of the rooms."

"What?" He seemed surprised.

"You didn't find her? She was in the tunnel next to yours, in a room with a wooden door. She is chained up to some awful, spikey board. I couldn't help her, Jake."

"Whoa, whoa, there are others down here? What the hell is going on?"

"I don't know. You said you found a way out? We have to get out of here and get help."

"Yeah, I'll show you. Come on."

Jake grabbed my wrist and led me away from the opening in the wall. I noted that we were moving diagonally from where I had emerged, trying to sear a mental image of it in my mind for the next time I could update my map.

As we walked along, I asked, "So, we are underground, right?" It was pretty obvious by the surroundings, but I hadn't really given it much thought until this moment, given everything else going on. I wondered how someone would build something so sadistic. I mean, even just the physics of it, never mind the intentions behind it. Like, how did someone dig all this out? Maybe it was an old mine or something and the killer was just occupying it with all his sick little traps. It wouldn't be farfetched I supposed, being that Pennsylvania is one of the largest mining states in the country.

"Yeah," he answered.

"How far down do you think we are?"

"About a half mile, maybe a little more."

Ok, that was pretty precise. Did he know where we were?

"How do you know that?" I questioned.

"I'll show you in a minute."

I was getting anxious. I mean, I was already anxious, but now it was exponentially worse. Being out of the loop sucked. The unknown was one of my least favorite things. I was going to say something to him, demand that he elaborate, but at that moment we dipped into another tunnel to the right, and what I saw had me stunned silent. There was light up ahead! Oh my God! There was light! We were going to get out of here!

"Jake ..." I started.

He interrupted, yanking hard on my wrist so we both fell against the wall. "Shh!"

What? Was the Bull Man up there? My heart began racing again. I scanned the tunnel ahead of us, quite a bit of which was at least dimly visible due to the beam of light pouring in from somewhere up ahead. I didn't see anything. Maybe Jake was just being cautious.

We listened for a second, and there was a weird,

repetitive clanging noise somewhere in the distance, like a hammer striking steel. It sounded pretty far away.

"What is that?" I wondered.

"No idea," Jake said. A few seconds later, he seemed to decide it wasn't a threat, and pulled my wrist again as he started to advance down the tunnel. "Come on," he instructed.

I clung to Jake's arm as we progressed further, and when we were nearly to the light source, Jake stopped. Randomly, a white beam of light stretched across the dirt floor in front of us, scanning left and right and revealing two precariously placed bear traps. Between them, only about the width of one person's shoulders allowed safe passage. I was disoriented and confused, and it took me a second to realize what was happening.

I was stunned once my brain caught up to everything. "You have a flashlight?" I asked. "Where did you get a flashlight?" Also, why hadn't he used it until now?

My suspicion of Jake was growing by the moment, and I started to feel like it would be prudent to keep a close eye on whatever he was doing. I was glad I hadn't told him I made a map. Between him getting the key unscathed, the flashlight, and everything else, my gut told me he might somehow be involved in everything.

He answered casually, "Found it in one of the rooms. Watch your step here."

Nervously, I watched Jake slip between the traps, then I followed his example and crept to the other side. Jake put the flashlight away and we continued into an area that opened up considerably in comparison to the low, narrow tunnels the maze had offered so far. We entered a circular room with two other tunnels connecting to it, one off to our left and one directly across from the one we were coming out of, and to my amazement, in the middle of the room was a bright white glow coming from directly above. When I tilted my head toward the light, I saw a small circle of blue about a half a mile above us. In this circle of blue, a single wispy cloud was drifting by.

"A well?" I guessed.

"That's what I was thinking. If I could get up there, to the opening I mean, I know I could chimney climb it."

"Ok, but how are we going to get up there?" The opening in the ceiling, what I imagined was once the bottom of the well, was at least ten feet from the ground, and there was nothing down here we could use to boost us up. If we could get up there, maybe we could chimney climb—but then I looked at my bandaged hands, still pulsing with pain, and wondered if I could really ascend that far with them in the condition they were. Jake was better off than me, but he had at least one hand damaged too. I wasn't so sure about this plan.

"What if I get on your shoulders? If I can get my upper body inside the well, I think I can lift myself up."

"No," I disagreed. "I don't think that's possible."

"Lani, we have to try."

"There's no way the Bull Man came down this well. There's another way out."

"But there's a way out right here, so why risk our lives going back in the tunnels?" Jake sounded incredulous, and I kind of didn't blame him. But I knew I was right. It was the same reason I didn't feel compelled to scream for help right then. The Bull Man, as elaborate and sick as he was, could have covered this well, and the fact that he didn't bother meant that it wasn't a threat to him. He knew that we couldn't escape from it, and he knew no one would hear us if we screamed. Well, no one except for him. The moment we screamed up that well he'd be upon us. I was sure of that much.

"It's not a way out," I burst his bubble. "It's false hope. He left it uncovered to taunt us."

Seeming annoyed, Jake replied, "Ok, well, you have a better idea?"

I thought about that for a moment before answering. Finally, I said, "Yeah. When I escaped my tunnel, I eventually went straight ahead, where the Bull Man came from. When I did, I almost fell in a spike pit, but in the middle of the pit was a bridge. I only got halfway across the bridge when I ran into him and had to turn around and run, and that's how I ended up being chased into the crack where you found me."

"Ok, so are you leading up to something? That doesn't sound like a plan."

"Well, when I went toward the bridge, the Bull Man had been behind me, near Cadence's room. So, how did he get in front of me on the other side of the bridge?"

Narrowing his brow, Jake considered this momentarily, but offered no response.

The thoughts were literally forming in my brain as I concluded my chain of reasoning, and then a lightbulb went off. "It means that somewhere back that way, where we just came from, there is another tunnel, where he would have come from, and that means that the tunnel in front of us must lead back to where I was. That's how he got in front of me, it has to be."

"That could be, but why does that matter?"

How could he not know?

"Because, Jake, it's where he comes from."

And wherever the Bull Man came from, I was certain there would be a way out.

20

My instincts were right again.

A little way further down the tunnel, with the aid of Jake's flashlight, we found the spike pits with the land bridge between them, and right beside the pit was a door.

"This is it," I said. "This is where he was coming from. I know it."

Grabbing the doorknob, I turned it carefully and pushed open the door. Jake shined the flashlight inside; left, right, up, and down. The coast seemed clear, so we went inside.

"We better be quick in here. If this is his room, he'll be back, right?" Jake reasoned. That was probably true. And as I looked around quickly, I could see this was undeniably the Bull Man's room. There was a twin bed in the corner, and an old beat-up easy chair on the opposite wall. There were tall metal shelving units packed with vacuum-sealed food, bottled water, and a plethora of other survival items. Sitting beside his bed was a little table with an unlit oil lamp, a book of matches, and a thick, worn-looking book with a piece of twine sticking out of its yellowed pages. On the floor next to the bed lay the brown burlap sack which he used to carry the items into our tunnels each time. A chill ran down my spine as I took it all in.

"I don't plan on staying," I said as I began shuffling around the room. "Just look for a way out. A trapdoor, a secret bookshelf, anything."

"Secret bookshelf?" Jake chuckled.

"Come on, stop wasting time. Give me the flashlight." I had no idea how he could laugh at a time like this. *Unless he was with the Bull Man.* Then he might find this pretty amusing. I panicked and turned around to see where Jake was and what he was doing. I had to keep tabs on him constantly, I reminded myself. Just in case. He was by the door, shining the light toward me, but his head was tilted back toward the tunnel. "What are you doing?" I pressed him.

"Keeping watch. Do you see anything?"

Keeping watch? I wondered if that was to alert me of the Bull Man or to alert the Bull Man of me. What if Jake knew I'd suggest coming here and he had some way to tell the Bull Man? Now, Jake was standing in the only exit and this room might have no other way out. I was making myself crazy.

I had to play it cool. So, I replied calmly, "Not yet. Can you give me the light? Or otherwise, I can keep watch and you look around?"

"Sure." He offered me the flashlight. I had been hoping he would take the second offer to let me stand guard so I could run if I needed to, but I couldn't outright show I distrusted him. I brought him one of the bottled waters from the shelf, took the flashlight, and continued my search.

I took a quick drink myself, then, moving quickly and precisely, I ran my hands along the walls, shined the light into every corner, tried pushing or lifting things, anything I could think of the find an exit. Nothing. Well, no way out anyway. I found a ring of keys on an old work bench next to a mallet, the same mallet I suspected he'd used to crucify me, and several other tools cluttering the area. When I was sure Jake was looking the other way, I carefully slid the keys into my pocket. One of them had to be for the exit, which I assumed would be locked when we did find it.

Another thought occurred to me: if Jake *was* involved, and we found the exit, would I have to fight him? Would it be better to stay behind Jake, that way I could stab him if I sensed anything off? Then I wondered if I even would sense anything. If Jake were working with the Bull Man, chances were good he was leading me around places where he knew the exit wasn't. That would mean the likelihood of the exit being on the side of the maze we were on now was much slimmer. All of that could be true, or none of it. I decided the most important thing was to maintain a cool head and observe carefully, and when new opportunities arose, act quickly.

"I don't think the way out is here after all," I admitted after a thorough search of the room.

"I told you. We should try to get up the well," Jake insisted. "We should get back there before he comes back."

I took one last scan across the floor and the back wall, and I caught a glimpse of the shoes the Bull Man had offered me. *Oh, what a gift!* I had to take those. I'd actually stand a chance without bare feet.

I went back over there and was putting the shoes on when Jake said, "Lani, let's go."

"One sec."

When I had the shoes on and laced, I grabbed two of the water bottles and some of the vacuum-sealed bread and tossed them into the Bull Man's sack. I twisted the top and bunched the fabric up in my fist, then slid the book of matches into my pocket and went back to the door.

"You should turn off the light," Jake suggested.

"Good idea."

I clicked the flashlight off and followed Jake out of the room. Jake went a few steps ahead as I quietly closed the door.

Jake whispered, "When we get back to the well ..."

But he never finished that sentence.

The Bull Man's silent but deadly steel came whirling around the corner, decapitating Jake instantly and crashing into the stone wall with such force it echoed all through the tunnels around me like lightning splitting a tree.

    I screamed bloody fucking murder.

21

I'd never seen anything so sudden and so gruesome in my life. The Bull Man bellowed his death call as Jake's body thumped on the ground and the head fell right after. I'd never forget the sound of his head plopping down and rolling in the dirt. But there was no time to process it.

Turning toward the bridge, I clicked on the flashlight and ran for my life. The axe scraped along the stone and the Bull Man roared after me again as he began the chase. I was much faster this time, now that I had the flashlight and the shoes. But the Bull Man was just as fast, and judging by what he had done to Jake, he wasn't toying with me this time. We had found his stash and he was pissed.

I found the T-junction and dove to the right, heading back to where I thought the crevice was where I hid the first time. It was too small for the Bull Man, so I knew I'd be safe in there.

By the time I got to the four-way intersection, he was right upon me. I looked over my shoulder for the briefest second and I saw him just a couple feet behind me, winding up to swing his axe at me. I sprinted forward and managed to duck into the tunnel to the right as the big axe swung over me and crashed into the ground in the middle of the intersection.

Enraged, the Bull Man growled, picked up his axe, and continued his pursuit. I beat him to the crack in the wall, but not by enough. I threw the burlap sack ahead of me into the wall, and I was most of the way inside when he swung the axe horizontally, hoping to deliver to me the same fate as Jake, but instead, he only got my shoulder as I slipped into the wall.

I cried in agony as the already blood-soaked steel buried itself a quarter inch into my flesh before grinding off the rocks and retracting. I reached for my shoulder, scurrying further back into my haven far enough to evade the Bull Man's tantrum of slashes upon the cracked wall. After a few terrifying seconds of him doing this, he let out an angry snort, dragged his axe across the stone as he had many times before, and vanished back into the maze. I shined my flashlight after him and watched him round the corner at the intersection just to be sure he was gone. Then, I put the light away, laid my head on the wall in front of me, and cried.

What was I going to do?

I was literally in such shock I couldn't do anything except try to block out the image of Jake's head rolling off the axe and tumbling across the ground.

No idea how long I was just sitting there.

Whenever it was that I finally started processing things, I realized two things. First, Jake wasn't with the Bull Man. That was pretty obvious at this point. I still couldn't believe it. Poor Jake ... The second thing was, I couldn't let the Bull Man catch me again. He could easily do so, which was now readily apparent, and the next time he did, I probably wouldn't be so lucky. I would have to try to gauge where he was and go around him, which would require much more precision than Jake and I had applied when going into the Bull Man's room.

That reminded me of the sack I had stolen, and I reached inside for one of the water bottles and a piece of bread. Slowly, I savored my precious lifelines as I thought more about everything. I wondered if Jake had been right about the well. Maybe that was the best way out. I could use one of the shelving units in the Bull Man's room to get up there and chimney climb the rest, like Jake said. No, no, that was ridiculous. I'd never move those shelves without alerting him, and even if I did, there was the same problem I had with climbing out of that well in the first place, which was that I wasn't actually sure I could chimney climb that far up in my current state.

I was back to square one.

All I wanted was to go home. I could feel the tears coming again.

I had to keep myself calm, so I decided to take a step back and make a mental list of things I could control, reminding myself of what I said in the very beginning: I had to stay positive and goal oriented. If I didn't, my head would be rolling in the dirt next.

Lani, you are not going to die.
You are not going to die.
You are not going to die.

I took a deep breath. The first thing I could control was my knowledge of the maze. I finished eating and took out the little piece of paper, unfolding it and pressing it to the wall. I had enough fresh blood on my shoulder to moisten my finger and draw in more tunnels. When I had filled in everything I knew, I examined it for a moment. There were two sections of the maze I wasn't sure about. One was if I were to go left out the other side of the crack instead of going toward the well. There had been a tunnel there, but we didn't go into it. I suspected that was the tunnel from which the Bull Man had come when he cut me off at the bridge before. So, there was a chance that one merely circled back to the four-way intersection, but there could also be other junctions between the two known locations. The second unfilled area of the map was the section I had cut into at the end of Cadence's tunnel. I had only sat just inside of it while I drew the map, then I had run back toward where I found the spike pits. The way out could be in one of those two places.

When I thought about Cadence, I remembered the

key ring. One of those keys could be for her chains! If I could sneak past the Bull Man I could get her out! Once I had her, we would figure out which of the remaining tunnels led out.

    Ok.

    I could do this.

22

I had a plan, and I thought it was halfway decent. I knew if I was going to get Cadence, I needed a reliable way of knowing where the Bull Man would be in the maze. After listening for a while, I realized that I wasn't going to get it by staying in that crack. The jig was up now that we had been running around, and the Bull Man was no longer following his pattern of behavior from before. His movements were far less predictable, plus, whatever he was doing out there, I couldn't hear him at all. I couldn't risk going out there not knowing where he was. I would have to create a diversion.

Shimmying my way through the crack, I emerged on the side with the well and made my way along the wall. I could see the light from the well up ahead, which illuminated the way enough that I could be sure the Bull Man wasn't up there. I switched on my flashlight and rushed down the tunnel to where the two bear traps that Jake had shown me were. I scanned the ground until I found a decent-sized pebble, picked it up, and turned it over in my hand for a moment. As soon as I did this I would have five to seven minutes, I guessed.

Ok, here goes nothing.

The bear trap slammed closed as I chucked the

rock at the pressure plate, the sound of clamping steel echoing through the tunnels. To complete the ruse, I screamed as loud as my lungs would allow, being sure to twist my voice into as tortured a sound as I could muster. Any moment now the Bull Man would come to feast on his prey, but by then I'd be on the other side of the maze.

I moved as fast as I could back through the crack, which was much faster with the flashlight to see where the razor blades were, and ran through the intersection and down the tunnel to Cadence's chamber. The whole time, I counted in my head. *One one-thousand, two one-thousand* ... I was up to a minute and a half when I arrived at Cadence's door. There was still plenty of time if the Bull Man had fallen for my trick.

"Cadence," I whispered as I slid inside the door. She didn't answer. I shined my flashlight at the back wall where she was chained and saw that she was slumped over, dead weight on the chains, with her head drooping. "Cadence!" I repeated with more urgency. Avoiding the trap in the middle of the room, I made my way over to her. I picked up her head to see her eyes closed. *No, no, please don't be dead!*

I pleaded one more time as I stroked her face, "Cadence, wake up, please."

Finally I got through to her and she awoke in a fit of gasping.

"Cadence, you're ok. I'm here. You're ok. I found

the key. I'm gonna get you out," I promised, reaching into my pocket for the ring of keys.

"Lani?" She was still in a daze. I started trying keys on her lock and she came around to realize what was happening. "Lani, you came back."

"Of course I came back. I would never leave you."

"How did you get the key?"

"From his room, it's a long story."

"Do you know the way out?"

"Working on that. I drew a map."

"A map? Of what?"

"Got it!" I said as the fourth key I tried freed her wrist at last.

"Oh God, thank you! Lani, I'm so glad you came back."

"Shh!" I warned her, making my way to her other wrist. "Almost out." A few seconds later, I had her other wrist free, and at last she descended from the spike rack.

Falling into my arms, she said, "Thank you, Lani. For coming back for me."

I smiled and hugged her so tightly I heard her breathe escape. Her back was soaking wet, covered in sweat and blood. Between tore bits of her shirt, I could feel blood dripping from open wounds. In my head, I was thinking that I shouldn't have been wasting time, but I couldn't let her go. I was just so glad to see her alive. I would have never forgiven myself if I had left her behind and she ended up dead.

When I was done embracing her I said, "Come on, let's get the hell out of here."

I led Cadence out of the room and down the tunnel, the way I had gone the first time I left her chamber and hid from the Bull Man. This was one of the unfilled sections of the map, and more importantly, the opposite direction from where the Bull Man would be if he took my bait.

"You said you have a map?" Cadence whispered as I took her wrist and guided her around the corner. We stopped there for a moment, where I had first conceived the idea to draw the map, and I took out the little piece of paper and knelt down so I could spread it out on the ground.

"This is the best I got," I replied. "These are the tunnels I know. I don't know where this one goes." As I explained, I shined my flashlight ahead, seeing that this tunnel seemed to go on for quite a bit longer than I expected, so far that I couldn't see another wall at the end where a junction might be. Nothing but blackness lay at the edge of my beam of light. I quickly realized what I was doing was a bad idea and directed the light back to the map, where its glow could do significantly less to give away our position.

"How many tunnels are there?" Cadence asked.

"I don't know. Like I said, I only filled in the ones

I'm aware of."

"And you haven't seen a way out?"

"No, nothing." Technically I had, but I didn't consider the well a real way to escape, and we didn't have time to be burdened with that conversation.

"So, what do we do?"

Looking at her bare, roughed-up feet, I asked, "How hard is it to walk?"

"It's fine. I'll be ok."

I wasn't so sure. Now that I had a second to assess her, that psycho had really done a number on her. She had been on that spike rack for at least six hours since I'd first seen her, and I had no idea how long it had been before that or what else she'd gone through. I knew how hard it was with bare feet, having tried to run from the Bull Man like that before, and she looked a lot weaker than I had been. If the Bull Man found us, I wasn't confident she could outrun him. What was I going to do then? It didn't matter, I decided, because I definitely wasn't leaving her behind. We'd just have to figure it out. No matter what, we were both getting out of there alive.

"All right, then. Let's go."

23

It took us about a minute or so to find the next junction when we ventured down the tunnel, and this one had two directions to choose from. The first led us rather quickly to a dead end, where the flashlight revealed a dozen long, wooden spikes protruding from the wall in front of us. I placed my hand on Cadence's chest and she gasped lightly, careful to remain quiet. I took her wrist and led the way down the other direction, where we went on for a bit before coming to another wooden door, like the one that had led to Cadence's torture chamber. Further into the tunnel, beyond where the door was, seemed like another dead end at first, until the light scanned over a crack in the wall.

The silence was absolute insanity. I couldn't believe that I hadn't heard a sound from the Bull Man since I tripped the bear trap. He must have realized he was tricked. If that was the case, he was probably lying in wait somewhere. Near the exit, if I had to guess. My heart started to race just thinking about him popping out of the darkness and chopping off our heads like he had with Jake. The image of the head rolling in the dirt played in my mind again, over and over. I seriously couldn't imagine how I was ever going to be the same again. Even after I escaped that place, I didn't know if I could ever forget.

Needless to say, when Cadence finally spoke, it was a welcomed reprieve from the terrors in my mind. "You think someone else is in there?" she wondered, staring at the door.

"Only one way to find out."

I gently placed my hand on the doorknob and turned, but the knob refused to move.

"It's locked?"

"I guess," I said.

"You think this is the way out? It has to be, right?"

Maybe. After all, why would the Bull Man leave the door to his own chamber unlocked, with all the goodies and keys to our chains, but not this one? If there was another prisoner in there, then why had he locked that one up and not Cadence? I stopped myself for a second, almost laughing inside; there was no point in trying to make sense of what a serial killer does. All of this was random. That was the point.

Despite my opinion, I didn't want to crush her hope. Instead I replied, "Maybe. Here, try the keys. I'm gonna check out this wall."

"Good idea."

I handed her the ring of keys and walked over to the crack in the wall. This one was smaller than the other one, barely large enough for me to shimmy through it. If there were razor blades in this one, I wouldn't be able to avoid them. That is, if this crack even went anywhere. As I shined my light into it and peered through the narrow space, something clicked. The Bull Man couldn't have put those razor blades in the other crack. He was too big to fit. That meant he had an accomplice for sure. Was the accomplice someone I knew? Maybe that was how the Bull Man got me down here. The note ... "I'm closer than you think" ... that had to be what it meant. I'd spent enough time thinking about it throughout this ordeal, and I just couldn't come up with any other explanation.

"These aren't working," Cadence whispered.

"Why am I not surprised?"

The more I looked into it, the more I wasn't confident the crack went anywhere. All I could see was darkness. This crack either went on forever or I was staring at a wall beyond the crevice. Either way, not an option.

As I went back over to Cadence I dug out the paper to update the map. When I unfolded it, it opened to the side with the Bull Man's note.

"What's that?" Cadence asked.

"Nothing ... this was what was on the paper when he left it."

I flipped the note over, intending to ignore it and try to figure out where we hadn't gone yet. There was only one section of the tunnels I hadn't been to, and it was a long way from where we were. The thought of crossing those tunnels where the Bull Man was likely to be made my entire body shiver.

Then Cadence asked something that changed everything.

"What's closer than you think? What the fuck does that mean?"

The light went on.

Maybe I just needed to hear someone say it out loud to get out of my own linear thought pattern. I don't know what it was, but the second she said it, I just knew.

The kidnapper was not closer than I thought.

The exit was.

24

"Cadence, I know where to go!" I declared, my hands on her shoulders and my eyes wide with realization.

"You know the way out?" She seemed excited, but unsure.

"Yes, I promise; I think I know what it means. We have to go back."

"What? But he is back there."

Images of Cadence on that rack, with her back arched, and blood and tears staining her face came to mind. My heart sank and my expression shifted to pure empathy. "I know he is, but we can't go this way, and we will sneak past him. I know the tunnels now. Trust me."

"I do trust you, but Lani, I can't see him again. I can't."

"I know. It's ok. I promise I'm gonna get us out, you hear? We are gonna be safe, but first, we have to be brave."

I could see her shaking already. Tears formed in her eyes. "No, Lani, I can't."

"You can," I said, wiping tears and stray hairs from her face.

".... No."

I pulled her close and let her cry for a second

while I held her. Cadence had been here for God only knew how long. For everything I'd been through, she'd been through it ten times over. I one hundred percent understood her fear of the Bull Man, but I also knew that we had to fight through that if we were going to beat him. The thing was, I was never great at saying that shit. If my sister were here she'd know how to comfort her. Me, on the other hand, I was always focused on the task at hand. Even at that moment I was thinking of our next move. If my assumption was right, the exit was in my tunnel, "closer than I thought." That meant we'd have to figure out where the Bull Man was, because we would need to divert him again so that when we went down my tunnel we'd have time to either find the exit or get the hell back out if I was wrong. I wasn't going to be wrong, though. That was what the note meant. That's exactly the kind of demented thing the Bull Man would do, is put the exit right next to me. The only thing I wasn't sure about was exactly where in my tunnel it would be, because I had been pretty thorough in searching around me when I was chained up. I was pretty sure there hadn't been any doors in the tunnel I started in, either. There was one place I hadn't looked, and it made total sense, given that we were underground; the door might've been on the ceiling.

"Cadence, we have to go," I said.

She lingered a bit longer in my embrace before asking, "You promise we are gonna be ok?"

"I promise." I stroked her hair again before letting her go.

"Ok. I'll follow you, Lani."

"Just do what I say. It'll be ok."

Taking her wrist, I let my thumb rub back and forth on her hand, trying my best to comfort her. Of course, there was no way I could promise that. Jake had promised me the same thing and look where he was. But I wanted Cadence to believe it. I wanted to believe it. We had to believe in something, *try something*, or else we were already dead anyway.

For several minutes I led Cadence back the way we had come. This time, I left the light off and used the wall to guide us. I already knew there were no traps in this hall, and I still hadn't heard the Bull Man, so for all we knew he could be lurking anywhere, waiting for us to give ourselves away.

When we got back to the tunnel where Cadence's chamber was, I stopped at the corner and pressed my hand to Cadence's chest. She understood I wanted her to wait and stood silently against the wall while I bent down and peered carefully into the tunnel, ensuring my head was well below axe level. I didn't expect to see anything besides darkness, but the important thing was whether I *heard* anything.

Nothing.

I waited a few seconds to be certain I wasn't

about to be decapitated, my heart pounding the whole time, then I led Cadence around the corner.

We crept along with no incident until we got to Cadence's chamber, where I saw the door was open a crack. I explicitly remembered closing it after Cadence and I escaped.

I squeezed Cadence's hand, and with my other hand, pointed to the cracked door. She put her hand over her mouth at the sight of it. That confirmed it. She remembered it being closed as well.

I had to make a decision. Was he in there, or ahead of us? Whichever one I decided could mean life or death.

Ok.

That bear trap was in there. If I busted the door in, I could throw my weight at him and knock him into it. But would his axe get me first? My mouth felt so dry, and my body was shaking so bad I thought my legs were going to collapse.

Come on, Lani! Make a decision!
Forward or back?
Go in there or no?
Cadence is depending on you!
Fight or flight?

I closed my eyes for moment and took a deep breath. Then I decided.

"It's a trick," I whispered.

"What?" Cadence asked, horrified.

"Let's keep going."

I decided it was either the door was booby trapped, or the act of opening or closing the door would tell the nearby axe-murderer where we were. It was how he was, with this cat-and-mouse sort of game. In fact, I thought there was a good chance he wasn't even near that door, and he had only left it open to mess with us.

But we hadn't even gone two steps beyond the door when that theory went to hell.

A violent roar shattered the silence around us, and a whoosh of air swept past me as the wooden door flew open. I didn't need to look behind me to know what was coming out.

"Run!" I screamed at Cadence.

"Lani!" she managed before she burst into tears.

I yanked her arm hard and took off as fast as I could, turning the flashlight on in front of us. The Bull Man's war cry echoed through the tunnel again as he began his chase.

"Lani! I can't!" Cadence cried, her words barely discernible. I felt her struggling, her weight tugging on my arm as I picked up speed. Shit! She didn't have shoes! We couldn't outrun him with her barefoot. Just as I had this thought, I felt her whole body yank my arm, causing me to stumble forward and lose my grip on her for a moment. I spun around and shined the light toward

Cadence, to see she had fallen, and right behind her the Bull Man was winding up his axe.

25

"No, no! Please, don't!" Cadence screamed. "I don't wanna die!"

That didn't matter. The Bull Man was going to kill her, the same way he decapitated Jake. Unless I did something.

Shining the flashlight in the Bull Man's face, I scurried toward him, scooping up a medium sized stone and throwing it straight at his head. It was the only thing I could think of on the spot, but thank God, it worked. I nailed him right in the eye! The Bull Man staggered, crying out in discomfort and momentarily taking one hand off the axe. It was enough time to get out of the killing zone.

"Cadence, come on!" I exclaimed, helping her to her feet. I pulled her up onto my shoulders and she wrapped her arms around me. "Hold this!" I handed her the flashlight so I could hold onto her legs as I ran. Cadence pointed the flashlight ahead. The light bounced wildly along the walls as we went.

"Lani, you have to run faster!" Cadence said.

"I'm going as fast as I can!"

"He's catching us!"

I could hear the Bull Man's angry grunting and his

thunderous footsteps slamming into the dirt, getting closer by the second. *Come on, Lani! Push yourself! You can go faster! You are a two-time state track and field champion. You can run a two-hundred meter in twenty seconds. No quitting!*

"Come on!" Cadence yelled. I veered around the corner of the four-way intersection, toward my tunnel, and with everything I had in me, pushed myself to accelerate. My vision was as straight as the tunnel through which I rushed, blocking out everything except the notion of where to go next. We had to lose him somehow. The only choice I had was to run across the land bridge and back toward the well.

We were right there, at the T-intersection, and Cadence again screamed, "Lani!"

I decelerated just enough to make the corner, but before I turned, I felt a heavy weight slam into my back. My shoulders bent forward, my spine curved, and Cadence made an awful gurgling sound, as if she had spit up a mouthful of seawater. I tumbled to the ground, Cadence falling on top of me as I fell into the dirt. The flashlight fell from Cadence's hand and rolled just out of reach ahead of me. Desperately, I kicked and crawled my way out from under her and dashed forward. I picked up the flashlight and shined it back toward the Bull Man. He roared with triumph as I shined it in his face.

"Cadence! Come on!" I exclaimed, extending my

hand to my downed friend. Then I shifted the light onto her, and what I saw was almost as horrific as Jake's tumbling head. Sticking out of Cadence's now limp, devastated body, was the Bull Man's big iron axe.

My mouth fell wide open and my knees bent inward and threatened to give way as I screamed in total horror. It felt like my whole body was electrocuted. The shock and fear and just ... pure disbelief overtook me, as if I'd woken from a vivid nightmare. I tried to run, but the Bull Man got me first.

I felt his unnaturally large hand clamp down on my forearm and yank me backward, and I began writhing and squirming furiously. If he was going to get me, I wasn't going to make it easy. His other arm wrapped around my chest, and he began lifting me. Knowing that if I let him lock his grip around me I was dead, I reflexively cocked my head back as hard as I could and headbutted the big man right in the chin. I felt the bull head shift upon impact, and the man let out an irritated grunt while loosening his grip on me. I must have hit something under there. Seizing the opportunity, I thrust my head back again, further dislodging the bull head, and kicked at his knees until I felt his grip loosen enough that I was able to squirm free.

Obviously seething, the Bull Man roared at me again and got ahold of my shirt before I could flee.

"Let me go!" I screamed.

While I was thrashing around against the Bull Man's grip, the already partially torn Henley ripped halfway off my torso. He grabbed my wrist and tugged my arm so hard I thought for sure it would be dislocated. He pulled me toward him and moved aside, allowing my momentum to send me crashing hard against the stone wall. My body bounced off the wall and the Bull Man caught me under my arms and lifted me up off the ground, slamming me down on my back and knocking the wind out of me. I coughed and gasped for air, and it felt like my spine had been struck with a sledgehammer. I could see the man fumbling with the bull head. I must have knocked it out of place or something.

My head fell to the side. The flashlight had fallen on the ground in such a way that I could see the axe still sticking out of Cadence's back. The light just grazed by her face, but it was enough to see the fear frozen on Cadence's face, fear she had taken to her tormented grave. *Oh, Cadence!* It was my fault! I promised her it would be ok, I talked her into coming back this way. I could feel myself about to cry as I stared into her cold, lifeless eyes. But then I snapped to.

I was still fighting for my life!

When I realized this, I flipped over to my knees and tried to run back down the tunnel where we had come from, toward the intersection where I could escape to the crack where I knew the Bull Man couldn't fit. I just barely made it to my feet when I felt him grab my ankle and rip my feet right back off the ground. My chin slammed hard despite my trying to break my fall. The psycho huffed with frustration and dragged me across the dirt toward him.

"No! Let go of me!" I screamed frivolously.

As my body came to a stop at the man's feet, he released my ankle and went for the axe in Cadence's back. Immediately, I turned onto my back, pulled my feet up, and kicked as hard as I could with both feet at the man's groin.

A direct hit!

The man staggered back until his back fell against the wall, holding his hands between his legs and groaning in pain. Once again, I grabbed the flashlight and set off toward the crack, but my attack didn't stave him off for long.

I heard his furious footsteps and his aggravated bellowing just feet behind me as I reached the intersection. Oh God! I was almost there! *Just a little more, Lani!*

I rounded the corner and made a full sprint for the crack. My body was going on full adrenaline, my heart pounding so hard it was deafening. I was just inches away.

Then, *thump*.

The man's big haymaker slammed me into the wall. I got my arms up to my chest just in time to stop my face from hitting the wall full speed. Still, I hit hard enough to be dazed, and I lost track of myself for a few seconds while I crumbled to the dirt. I felt him grab my ankle again and start to drag me along on my back. This time, I was too beaten down to struggle. For a good ten seconds or so, the whole way from the crack to the intersection, I let him drag me in that way, where my body felt so dead I might as well have already been in a body bag. My life started flashing before me. My dad, my sister, all the moments in my life I felt most safe. I pictured Ginny and I playing in the dirt lot at the end of our road with all the neighborhood kids. I saw my dad, back when he was happy with my mom, handing us Christmas presents. Even my first kiss with Allison Stone, by an old tree next to the basketball courts. The sun was in my face, and I closed my eyes too early I think, because she kind of laughed at me. She brushed her hair back and leaned into me, and her lips tasted like Pina Colada chewing gum. Later that summer, my dad took my family to the Bahamas. That was our last vacation together, before my mom blew everything up. All these memories were flipping around in my brain, mixing together in fuzzy, momentary clips, like compilation videos of my life. I think I knew what people meant by seeing the light now. It was kind of like that, in the sense that I felt out of body, and everything was faraway, echoing almost. I didn't literally see white light, but I saw little flashing silver things. I felt like I wasn't a part of reality. My God, I never thought I'd miss those moments in my life so much. I'd taken so many things for granted. If I ever saw my dad and sister again, I was going to hug them forever.

It was when the Bull Man started turning around the corner, back to where the axe was, that I realized where I was again.

"No! No!" I started kicked my feet and flipped onto my stomach. Reaching out at the wall, I gripped the corner of the tunnel and tried to pull myself away from the Bull Man. This only seemed to annoy him, and he easily yanked me free. Now, he picked up the pace, dragging my bare stomach across the rocky dirt. I couldn't do anything about it except kick and scream and try to find something to grab. I held my chin up because I had this fear that he'd drag me over a rock and it would cut my neck open. The whole way down that tunnel, I was racking my brain, trying to think of something to do, anything to do other than letting the Bull Man drag me back to that axe and split me in half. If only I'd went for his axe instead of running before, maybe I could have killed him.

Wait a second ... *the spike!*

26

Thank heavens for the spike! It was still there, where I'd dropped it! I felt the thin metal shaft roll across my stomach as he dragged me over it, right before he deposited me next to Cadence's body. The second he let go of my ankle, I felt his big, heavy boot press down on my back. Horrendous squishy noises filled my ears as the Bull Man wriggled his axe trying to liberate it from Cadence's flesh. I had to act fast.

Just as I heard the wet, popping sound of the axe leaving her body, I grabbed hold of the spike and thrust my arm back as hard as I could, and stabbed the Bull Man straight through the calf. He cried out in agony and fell onto his back, the axe falling to his side.

Scurrying to my feet, I turned to see the Bull Man already unsheathing the spike from his flesh. My adrenaline took over. *It's now or never, Lani.*

Screaming at the top of my lungs, I rushed at him and kicked him in the face. He fell backward, the bull head shifting around on his neck as he bounced off the hard ground. The spike made a puttering noise as it fell into the dirt. "Fuck you!" I blared with all my might before I stomped on his groin with my heel. The man reeled with pain, crumpling his legs together and rolling to the side to protect himself.

While he squirmed about, I tried to lift the axe. With great effort, I would add—that was one heavy piece of steel. Out of the corner of my eye, I saw the tip of the spike in the ray of light cast by the flashlight, which lay on the ground nearby. Changing my strategy, I abandoned the axe and wielded the spike instead. Fresh blood dripped off the tip as I took it from the dirt.

The man rolled over and lunged to his knees just in time to meet the spike as I drove it into his thigh. This time I got a full scream from him, though it was muffled by the bull head. I pulled the spike from his thigh, continuing to scream and curse at him as I began moving my arms up and down as fast as I could. Up, down, up, down the spike went, splattering blood all over my arms, chest, and face amid the brutal gorefest. I'm not sure how many times I stabbed him, nor even what I was stabbing for that matter. I just lost my mind; let it all come out. All my anger, sorrow, rage, everything, I channeled through that spike.

He threw his arms up, trying to protect his body from my attack, but I didn't relent. In my fury, I felt the spike slice, cut, and impale his arms, all while the man wailed in pain and tried desperately to crawl away from me. He kicked at my chest but deterred me for only a moment. When I heard him shuffle in the dirt, I drove the spike into his leg again, then slammed my knees onto his chest, pinning him to the ground.

Somehow, despite all the damage I had caused, the man caught me under the armpits and launched me off him. He lunged toward me, grabbing my wrist and slamming it against the wall. I dropped the spike.

"No!" I screamed as he reached for my neck. No way I was letting him get ahold of me again. "Get off me!" I squirmed away from his grip and slid around the man. He tried to react, to grab my shoulder, but he was much slower than me, injured, hindered, weak. I knew this was it. I had the upper hand for once, and I was going to finish it.

Spinning around and picking the spike up from the ground, I buried it in his calf. He tumbled painfully to the ground and rolled onto his back, reaching for his freshly impaled leg just in time to see me with my hands on the hilt of the axe. For once, the Bull Man stopped cold. I had him, and he knew it. Then he surprised the hell out of me by speaking for the first time.

"Fucking bitch," he grunted, the bitterness of defeat lingering on his tongue. Those were the only two words he ever said to me before I split his chest open with the great steel axe.

27

My heart. Oh, my fucking heart! It had never beat so fast in my life, and when it was over, I felt like a plane in freefall. My mouth was open, but no sound would come out. I didn't know where to start. It was as if all my energy was being expended to contain the inexplicable cannonball of emotions begging to be released. I fell to my knees and let my hands off the axe as it lay, a stoic monument of violence buried deep in the Bull Man's flesh.

A wave of unconsciousness swept over me. I don't know how else to describe it. For however long it was, I felt out of body, with no idea what to do or say, but just knowing I felt something. And that something was bubbling beneath this consciousness, pulling me toward some other corridor of my mind I never knew existed. I was part of the darkness now. No matter what I did, I would carry this passenger forever.

I felt myself hunch over, and I started gasping for air. I couldn't breathe, it was like my heart was going a hundred miles an hour and someone pulled the e-brake. For several laborious moments I battled that feeling, until finally, I flew into a fit of coughing and puking. I started to feel all the aches and pains in my body again, especially my hands, which were absolutely throbbing with pain after exerting my injured limbs to kill the Bull Man.

Finally, when it was over, I let myself cry.

Poor Cadence ... Jake ... I couldn't save them. If only I'd listened to Cadence, maybe she'd still be alive. It was my fault. I couldn't block my thoughts any more than I could block the tears from flowing full force. How many people were going to be devastated when they learned about what happened? Lives would be changed forever. How many lives had been changed here in these tunnels before today? How was I going to tell Cadence's mom? As I contemplated this, I stroked Cadence's cheek and gently closed her eyes.

I'm so sorry.

I had to get out of here. Otherwise, they died for no reason.

With renewed resolve, I wiped the tears away and got to my feet. I ran my hands along my body, assuring myself I was alive. My shirt was gone. I had barely acknowledged it in the tussle with the Bull Man, but now I could feel my torso, slashed, cut, and bruised, all bare except my bra. But that was the least of my concerns. I was ok enough to walk out. It was going to be ok. That was the most important thing. Checking my pockets, I found I still had the keys and the matches in one pocket, and the map in the other. Hopefully, I wouldn't be needing the map. That was, if I was right about where the exit was.

Picking up the flashlight and the spike, I began down the tunnel where all this had started.

Please, let me be right.

I prayed the whole time I walked down my tunnel. The idea of having to search the maze again for an exit was overwhelming. Even with the urgency presented by the Bull Man gone, I wasn't sure I had the will to go back. All I wanted was for the exit to be up there, and for me to run out into the sun. I'd run all the way to my dad's house and jump into his arms. I didn't care how far it was. I wouldn't stop until I was home.

My flashlight revealed the metal block which had once bound me to this little corner of the maze. I stopped where I was and guided the light along the length of my former chains, then over the walls surrounding the area. I was intentionally waiting to check the ceiling, waiting until the very last second, when I had exhausted every other inch of my prison, verified that every crevice bore no chance of escape, just to hold onto hope for a little bit longer.

When nothing else remained, I let the light crawl up to the ceiling.

For the first few inches, nothing but dirt. A support beam came into view, crossing over the dirt and connecting to each wall with wooden triangular edges. More dirt. Another beam. Dirt. Then finally, a smooth, wooden surface, the shape of a square, and on one side of this square, right in the middle, was a handle.

The way out.

My heart started racing again, this time out of anticipation as I climbed up on the metal chain block and reached for the handle. To reach it, I had to stand on my tiptoes and throw my body out toward it. On my first couple of tries, I lost my balance and missed the handle. This was already a difficult task, and in my current state of exhaustion, it seemed impossible. Two failed attempts later, I decided to try to just jump up to it from the ground, thinking I could get more momentum that way. I did high jump a few times in track, so maybe I could reach it. Unfortunately, no such luck. All I got was my hand cutting through air.

There had to be a hook, I decided. Maybe back in the Bull Man's room? Or maybe he just used his axe. I had all but decided I had no choice but to go back in the maze to find something, but first, I wanted to try one more time from the chain block.

I made my way up, positioned myself as close to the edge as I could, and took a deep breath. All at once, I thrust myself up to my tiptoes and hurled my arms in front of me like I was Super Woman. My body started tumbling forward off the block when I felt the rough wooden handle graze my right hand. Clamping my hand as hard as I could, I caught my grip around the handle and tore open the door as I fell to the ground.

As my body fell beyond the length of the door, my hand slipped off the handle, tearing at my makeshift bandages and causing several splinters in the process. I yelped in pain as I hit the ground and clutched my freshly injured hand. I honestly couldn't imagine my hands taking any more punishment. But I sucked in a deep breath and pushed it aside. I was getting out! It was almost over!

Hurrying to my feet, I found that a rope had descended from the space beyond the trapdoor. When I pulled on it, a ladder came down into the tunnel, allowing me to climb up above my chain block.

When I reached the top of the ladder, I seemed to be in another tunnel. This one proceeded in an upward slope, seeming to get progressively more finished as I ascended. The path became worn and packed and the wooden beams closer together on the walls and the ceiling. I was getting closer to the surface.

That tunnel must have gone on for about a half mile, or at least, that's what it felt like. The path had leveled out for most of the way, until suddenly, it cut sharply uphill. My heart skipped a beat. A trapdoor rested at the top.

28

A basement. I was in a basement. My God, I was out of the maze!

I pulled myself up out of the tunnel, which had been dug out beneath the trapdoor and hidden beneath an area rug. It had taken me a couple of good shoulder smashes to knock the rug off, but at this point nothing was stopping me.

Working quickly but quietly, I searched the room for an exit. There were no windows, and no doors that I could see, but obviously there was an exit. This was how the Bull Man came and went; that much was obvious. So there was a way out somewhere.

I felt along the walls, pressing lightly as I went, looking for a hidden door or anything out of place. I found myself looking at the ceiling for answers. Then I noticed a handle stuck to the wall. Pushing on that part of the wall, I found that I could move the wall inward, and I did so until I felt it catch on something. For good measure I pushed one more time, but it was totally stuck. That was fine, because I could see light on the other side. The wall had pushed in so I could see the inside of it was hollow, and so was the area behind the wall to my right. Hollow just enough so I could slink inside the wall and to the other side, where I came out in what looked like a normal basement.

There was sunlight!

Sunlight! Coming from a little rectangular window above a washer and dryer. I bet I could fit through that! I abandoned the flashlight on a little table next to a half-full laundry basket and climbed up on the dryer to examine the window. The dryer was in the middle of a cycle, and I could smell that fresh linen smell, feel the bits of steam escaping the vent. Instantly I thought of being a kid, thought of my mom letting me help her put stuff in the dryer. I pictured how Ginny and I used to sit inside the dryer and try to make it spin. All I wanted, desperately, was to see them again.

I ran my fingers along the metal framing that encased the windowpanes. Unfortunately the window was totally stuck, and the panes were so small that, even if I broke the glass, I couldn't fit through. I wanted to cry looking out at the sun shining over the cornfield. I was so close!

Looking around the room, I saw one other window near a tool bench, but upon inspection that window was no good either. My eyes went to the staircase. The only way out was through the house. White knuckling the spike in my right hand, I crept up the stairs. At the top I placed my hand on the brass doorknob and slowly turned it.

I pressed myself into the door and made my way

into the farmhouse. I came out in a hallway. To my left were the stairs to the second floor and I wasn't sure what else at the end of the hall, and to my right was the kitchen. On the far side of the kitchen was a door with a white latticed curtain over the solitary four-pane window. There it was. I was so damn close. I wanted to run for that door, but somehow I kept my composure. I reminded myself; *you're not out yet.* There might be someone else up here. The dryer was running, so it was very likely someone was, actually.

Clutching the spike ever more tightly in my hand, I carefully closed the basement door and crept along the whitewashed walls of the hallway toward the kitchen. Along the way I glanced at a photo hanging on the wall of what seemed like a normal, happy family. A mother, father, and two twin girls, both blonde, with their hair done up in matching braids. Another nearby photo showed the girls a little older, in basketball uniforms. Next was Dad in his policeman's attire. A cop? What the hell? These people couldn't be involved in the Bull Man's depravity, could they? No way. Especially not a cop.

Well, wait a second. There were plenty of dirty cops. Who is to say there weren't cop serial killers? There's plenty of cops guilty of killing innocent, unarmed people. There's bound to be a truly malignant one in the mix. It could be this one. After all, there was no way ... there was just no way he hadn't known what was in his basement.

Unless they'd just moved there or something. But no, even then, that would mean the killer allowed people to move into his established torture chamber. No way. These people would have been in the maze way before me if that was the case. These people were involved. Or at the very least, Dad was.

I got to the end of the hall and snapped myself to attention. I could figure all that out later, after I escaped. Peering around the corner, I saw the coast seemed to be clear, and I began tiptoeing across the kitchen toward the door. Any second, I was going to be out. I was literally three feet from the door when the worst possible thing that could occur in that moment happened.

The kitchen door swung open.

A middle-aged blonde woman entered the house with her arms full of groceries. Her keys dangled from her hand and her sunglasses were still on her face.

I froze.

"Danny!" the woman called as she stepped inside, kicking the door shut behind her.

"Honey?" I heard the man say from the couch.

Then she turned and saw me. For a split second, I don't think she knew what she was looking at. But she got wise quickly and let out a terrified scream, dropping her armful of bags onto the floor around her feet.

"Who are you? Why are you in our house?" the woman shouted. Now alerted, the man swung around the couch and into the kitchen, where he stood in the entryway. He was in plainclothes, but he still had his badge secured to his big leather belt. His badge, and his gun. His expression was meant to be shock, but I knew otherwise. This man had kidnapped me. He had to have been part of it. The moment I saw him, felt his presence, I knew it.

My heart was pounding. I should've run. I should have just fucking run. But I couldn't. On the man's hip was a nine-millimeter, and I knew he wouldn't hesitate to use it. The only reason he hadn't was because, clearly, his wife was unaware of his proclivities. Danny had been living a double life, and perhaps he didn't want to give that up. He thought maybe he had a chance to save face as long as he didn't give anything away.

On the spot, panicked, I said the first thing that came to mind to maintain the man's cover: "Please, help me! I was in a barn ... I don't know where!"

"Oh my God!" The woman covered her mouth with both hands, her face melting into tears of empathy.

"I ran away, this is the first house I saw. Please, help me!"

"Someone kidnapped you? Is he still after you?" The woman came over to me and examined my wounds. "Oh, God! You're still bleeding."

"I ran so far, through the woods." I started sobbing and leaning on the woman's arm. Danny looked at me with severity as his wife's back turned toward him. Tears rolled down my face, and only a fraction of it was the act. I was so close to being free, and yet I was in the crosshairs again.

Danny switched back to his concerned, confused face and hurried over to me. Kneeling down next to his wife, he looked at my bloody, mutilated body and asked, "What did this man do to you?" Turning to his wife, Danny added, "She is hurt real bad, Lisa."

"He stabbed me. Please, I just need a doctor," I pleaded.

As Danny reached out and touched my wrist, I flinched, raising the spike with my other hand. Lisa seemed taken aback, as if noticing the weapon for the first time. Shaking off my fear as best I could, I lowered the weapon.

Still kneeling beside us, Danny took my hand in his, examining my fingers and the dirty strip of fabric covering my stab wounds. I felt a fresh twinge of pain as he turned my wrist and the hole in my hand stretched. I winced and shut my eyes for a second, pinching off a fresh tear. With fake sincerity, he asked, "God ... who would do something like this?" His wife looked at him with the most devastated expression. Disbelief, sadness, empathy. She definitely wasn't part of any of it.

"I'm calling the police right now, this girl needs an ambulance," Lisa declared.

"Yes," Danny agreed. "I'll call. They'll come faster if I talk to them, light a fire under their asses. You run upstairs and get some gauze and rubbing alcohol."

"Ok, yes, I will. I'm gonna get you a shirt, too, ok honey?" The woman stroked my hair and the side of my face before starting down the hall.

"No!" I shouted instinctively. The woman stopped, looking confused. I couldn't be alone with him. The second I was, he'd kill me. The only reason he hadn't was because I'd covered for him. If I blew his cover, he'd probably shoot his wife and me, and if his wife left us alone, well, he'd just kill me and cover it up somehow. I couldn't bear the thought of either outcome.

"She'll be right back," Danny insisted. "You need medical attention."

"I just want to go home. What if the man is still after me? I don't want to stay here."

"Don't worry, help is on the way."

Danny's wife got irritated. "For heaven's sake, Danny, call them!"

"I am." He took out his phone and starting to dial. I don't know who he was dialing, but I knew it wasn't the police.

She started to walk away again, and I was desperate. I couldn't think of any good reason for her not to leave the room, and I was running out of time. Danny had the phone to his ear and someone picked up. I wanted so badly to scream into the phone for help, to tell whoever was on the other line that this man was an impostor, a killer masquerading as a beacon of justice. But I stopped myself. The moment his cover was blown there was nothing stopping him from ending it all in a hail of gunfire.

Lisa was about to go up the stairs, and I decided I didn't need to think of a good reason. It was reason enough that I was traumatized and irrational, having just endured days of torture and near-death. Jumping up from the kitchen floor, I rushed down the hall after Lisa, calling out to her, "Wait! I want to talk to Ginny!"

She turned around with a look of concern on her face and asked, "Who's Ginny?"

"My sister," I said, grabbing her hand with my free hand. "I want to call my sister. Please, I just want to go home."

I saw Danny poking around at the end of the hall, saying into the phone, "Yeah, Margret, I need you to listen to me. There's an emergency, I need you to ..." He waited a second, covering his other ear with his hand, like my voice was stopping his concentration. "Hold on." He cut around the corner back toward the living room.

He wasn't going to say it. His wife was almost out of earshot now. He was about to come up with some excuse and hang up, then he'd slit my throat the second his wife wasn't looking.

"Of course, honey. Here, use mine," Lisa said and went back into the kitchen to pluck it from her purse. She handed me that beautiful, lifesaving iPhone with its pearl pink, hard-plastic case, and I started to cry all over again as I slid the matching PopSocket between my fingers. She unlocked the phone for me and said reassuringly, "Danny is on with the police right now. Call whoever you need to. I am gonna get you some clothes and get you cleaned up, and I promise you, you're going to be ok."

"Thank you," I cried. "Thank you so much." I dialed Ginny's number and held the phone to my ear. *Please, pick up.*

Danny strolled back over to the end of the hallway and said to Lisa, "Margaret just dispatched three cruisers and an ambulance. They should be here in less than ten minutes."

Yeah right. Margaret didn't dispatch anyone, because he didn't tell her he had two murder victims in his basement and one near-death escapee in his downstairs hallway. Meanwhile, I was on three rings, and I was getting anxious as hell. *Please, Ginny, answer your phone!*

"I'm gonna be right back, ok?" Lisa said before starting up the stairs.

"Wait!" I called, ascending the stairs behind her. Four rings. *What the hell, Ginny? Please!*

"She'll be real quick," Danny assured me. "Come

on out here, I'll get you a washcloth. No reception upstairs, anyway."

"He's right," Lisa said. "I drop calls all the time. Crappy service out here. Your best bet, honestly, is to go outside."

The fifth ring started in my ear, and finally I heard my sister's voice. "Hello?"

"Ginny!" I couldn't help but scream.

"Lani?! Oh my God, where are you? Are you ok? We've been looking for you!" Ginny's voice became immediately urgent when she realized it was me calling.

"I'm on a farm, um, I don't know." I started panicking, realizing I had no idea where the house was located. Frozen on the stairs for fear of the call dropping if I moved, I yelled up the stairs to Lisa, "What's your address?"

"Lani? Lani, where are you?" Ginny was still frantically asking.

I heard Lisa reply, but I couldn't quite hear her. Danny answered instead, making his way down the hallway toward me. "Tell her to follow the sirens, they will be coming this way as we speak."

"Ginny! I'm outside of the city, on a farm, I was abducted. Please, call the police."

"Oh my God! Are you hurt?"

"I'm hurt bad, Ginny. I need help, please, bring the police."

"Where do I bring them? Lani, what's around you?"

My whole body tensed as Danny drew closer. I glanced at the phone, noticing it only had one bar. If I moved away from him I might lose Ginny. But if I let him get in range of me, anything was possible. I tightened my grip on the spike, turning my body so my back was against the wall and I could watch his movements.

He came around to the base of the stairs, his hand resting on the wooden sphere atop the base of the railing. Our eyes met the entire time. He wanted me dead, no doubt about it. The look in his eyes ... it was like a tiger waiting to pounce, waiting for the perfect moment to sink his teeth into my neck.

"I don't know, Ginny. I don't have service, just don't hang up," I said. Danny came up the first two steps, raising his hands in front of him as if to say he was innocent. I didn't buy it for a second. Raising the spike toward him, I said, "Stay there."

"Who are you talking to?" Ginny asked.

Danny spoke softly to me, "It's ok. I know you've been through a lot ..."

I talked over him to Ginny. "Write down the number I'm calling from! If I move, I might lose you. Ginny?"

"Yeah, I'm writing it down."

"Come into the kitchen," Danny requested yet

again. "Let me get you some water and a washcloth."

I shook the spike at him. "Stay back!"

"Lani? Oh God, hang on, ok?" Ginny pleaded. "I got the number. I'm calling the cops!"

Lisa appeared at the top of the stairs with clothes draped over her arm and a first aid kit. "Danny? What's going on?" she asked as she descended the stairs, staring questionably at the spike I was pointing at her husband.

"She's just scared," Danny reasoned. "I offered her to come sit and drink some water, and she just got spooked. Can't say I blame her. She's been through hell." No shit I'd been through hell, and he put me through it. Part of me considered just leaping at him, jumping down on him and driving the spike right into his skull, but I couldn't bring myself to do it. This wasn't an action movie. Knives didn't beat guns. And if I didn't kill him, not only would I be dead, but his innocent wife as well.

"Oh, you poor girl," Lisa practically sobbed, touching my shoulder gently as she stopped beside me on the stairs. "We aren't going to hurt you. I'm gonna get you clean, and you can put these on. Help is already on the way." Danny shot me a subtle look when he was sure Lisa's gaze was averted. His hand hovered near the nine-millimeter.

"It's ok Lisa, maybe we should just let her be?" Danny suggested. "Like you said, the police are on the way. She's obviously in shock. Might be better to leave her be until they arrive."

Ginny, still on the phone, was asking me if I was still there. My brain was starting to scramble. Sensory overload. Like, I wanted to reply to Ginny, but for just a few seconds I felt this whirlwind of emotions, so powerful and so mixed up I didn't know what I was supposed to do.

"Is that your sister?" Lisa said.

Realizing she was talking to me, I snapped to. "Oh, yeah."

"Lani?" Ginny seemed relieved. "I texted Dad, he's on the phone with the cops now. Can you give me any landmarks at all?"

"Here, I can tell her the address," Lisa offered, taking the phone from me. I flinched, fearful of the idea of giving up the reassurance of my sister on the other line, but I reacted too slowly, and Lisa already had the phone. Danny was still at the base of the stairs blocking us in. "Um, hello?" Lisa said into the phone. "Hello? Yes, you are Lani's sister? We have her—huh? Hello?" Lisa looked at the phone, then sighed and said, "This stupid house."

"Did it drop?" Danny asked, his face seeming to illuminate at the prospect of this.

"Yeah. I told you," she said, glancing at me. "The service is so spotty in here."

My heart started racing again. "I have to call her back," I begged.

"We will, honey. Come on, come sit down and let me clean you up, we'll call her again from the kitchen. Reception's better in there for some reason."

Putting her hand on my shoulder, Lisa guided me down the stairs. In the few seconds that we walked down those stairs I had a thought: there wasn't really an outcome where Lisa didn't die. Danny hadn't actually called the cops, because if he did, there was no way he could cover this up. When the cops went looking for the alleged barn I had come from, they wouldn't find it. When that search came up empty, they'd come back to Danny. My bloody shoeprints were all over the hallway, and my handprints all over the walls. There was no way the police wouldn't investigate this place. Damn! I realized then that I had opened a can of worms that I couldn't close back up. No matter what I did, Danny would still kill her, because as long as she was alive she would realize Danny hadn't called the cops and she would try to report what happened today.

But if that were true, why was Danny still playing this game? Had he not figured that out yet? Or maybe he was trying to fabricate something in his mind where he could keep his family and make it all go away. I didn't know what he was thinking, but regardless, I concluded that no matter how guilty I felt about it, I had to forget about Lisa. Whatever happened was going to happen. I had to live.

As we reached the base of the stairs, Lisa asked Danny, "Why haven't they arrived yet? Danny, I'm worried, you should call again."

"They are on the way. Any minute now," he said. "Lots of crazies in this town. Keeps 'em busy."

HOLY SHIT!

That's what he said to me, the night I was with Sami. He was walking around the side of the house with his flashlight, and he said, "Glad you called us. Lots of crazies in this town. Can never be too careful." It was him! Danny was the cop who showed up at my apartment that night with the fisherman! And my black, lacey bra, the reason I was wearing it now ... Sami ran back in because I asked him for clothes ... I told him to grab the ones I had on the dresser ... A pair of blue jeans and a gray Henley ... and he grabbed my bra off the floor ... I dressed quickly inside the entryway right before the cops came. That's when he got me. I passed out after. I couldn't remember anything after the cops left. Sami and I went back inside, to the couch, and ... that's when he offered to wait outside my house. That's how he got me!

My thoughts were so loud that Lisa's voice was almost an echo. "I don't know. What if that psycho is coming here after her? I think you should call."

I was hyper-focused on Danny, my eyes narrowed, my hand tight and ready on the spike. His jaw shifted uncomfortably, and after a brief pause he replied, "All right, yeah, I'll call Margaret." Finally, he moved aside enough for Lisa and me to pass him into the hallway. This fucker, he did all this to me. He drugged me, dragged me here, murdered my friends ... there was no way he was about to let me walk out of there.

"Ok, honey, it'll be over soon. We'll just—"

Damn right it would be over soon.

No more contemplating.

With a surge of pure adrenaline, I stabbed Danny right in the thigh as hard as I could. He screamed in agony and fell to the floor, and by the time he hit the wooden floorboards I was already running down the hall.

"Danny!" I heard Lisa behind me.

In three seconds flat, I was at that kitchen door. I turned the door handle and stepped out into the sun, and the second my feet hit the ground outside I sprinted as fast as my legs could take me. I never looked back. Even when I heard him screaming, heard the sound of his gun firing, I never stopped, and I never turned around. I ran and ran for at least a half a mile across that farm. Through the hills, the pumpkin patch, and the cow fields. Into the cornfield and past the granary.

When I finally reached the road, I ran out to the center line and started doing jumping jacks, waving frantically at an oncoming car.

"Hey! Stop, please! Help me!" I screamed.

The driver slammed on the brakes, and I

scrambled to move out of the way as the car came to a stop right in front of me. Tripping over myself, I fell to my hands and knees on the blacktop beside the vehicle.

"Oh my God! Are you ok? What happened to you?" A woman cried as she flew open the door and rushed to my side. She called to her husband as he came out the passenger's side, "Brad, we have to get her to a hospital!"

"How bad is she bleeding?" Brad wondered. He ran around the front of the car and knelt beside me as the woman grabbed my arms and lifted me to a sitting position.

She cradled me in her arms. "It's ok, sweetie You are gonna be ok, you hear?"

"He has a gun," I sputtered, pointing over the hill toward the farm. I couldn't manage anything else besides coughing and bursting into tears.

"What? Who has a gun?" she asked. I couldn't answer. All I could do was stare wide-eyed at the cornfield, hyperventilating in fear. Any second, I expected Danny to burst through the stalks and start shooting. I could barely breathe. I was so exhausted and full of urgency.

"I'll call 911," Brad said. "Should we get her out of the road?"

"I don't know. Just call the ambulance. Hurry!" she replied.

"Right, ok."

By now, a car that had been coming the opposite direction had pulled over and the people got out of the car to see what was going on. I was so delirious; everything was starting to feel out of body. I vaguely recall hearing Brad talking on the phone, but I had no idea what he was saying. Then I started to realize that Danny wasn't coming. He was injured, and I had run so far, and there were too many people now. But what about Lisa? What about those two daughters? There were still so many things in my brain I couldn't reconcile, but it didn't matter then. All I knew was that it was over. I was safe. I could stop being afraid.

My crying slowed, but mainly because I was on the verge of passing out. Now that my adrenaline was wearing off, my body felt like it was shutting down. I remember the woman cradling me in her arms, holding me close to her chest, and she told me her name was Emily, and that help was on the way. After that, I heard sirens in the distance, and everything else was like a lucid dream. The ambulance and cop cars showed up and I saw the paramedics rushing over to me.

"Lani! Oh, thank God!" I heard my dad's voice. I couldn't even see him yet, but I put my arms out to hug him. "It's ok, baby. It's ok, you're safe now," he spoke softly to me as he took me from Emily's arms. I'd never been so grateful for anything as I was of my dad's embrace, for his strong, loving hands stroking my back, making me feel safe.

"Move aside, sir," a paramedic said.

"Dad," I muttered as they tore me away from him.

"It's ok, I'll be with you the whole time."

I remember bits and pieces after that, but not much. I know the paramedics loaded me onto the gurney, and my dad was standing over me, looking down at me, stroking my face.

"Where's Ginny?" I asked him.

"She's coming. Don't worry about anything, just breathe, ok?" my dad said.

I think I just smiled at him and then, it was all a blur. I heard the ambulance doors close, felt them pull away, and that was it. I was free. It was finally over.

I was alive.

Bottom of the Well

After

A lead vein. That whole goddamn maze started because some farmers were selling lead to make bullets. Pennsylvania was at the heart of many conflicts during the Civil War, and after the war, a major hub for mining strategic materials for railroads and other new industrial projects. Needless to say, anyone who found lead, copper, coal, or any other industrial resource on their property was doing pretty well for themselves back then. Fast forward to modern day, and a lot of those mining operations are abandoned, leaving plenty of space for people like Danny to set up his twisted labyrinth. I still found it hard to believe, but that's what happened, according to the history of the farm.

Why did I look it up? I had to know. I couldn't just let it go without knowing. But it took some time. Months passed after the day I escaped from that hell before I finally found the mental strength to go back and analyze what had happened to me. It took a lot of therapy, trust me, and even still I'll never be the same. My therapist told me I would probably have PTSD for my entire life, and it wasn't something to try to run away from or hide away, but instead, something to manage and cope with. It made sense, but I felt like I needed something a little more. I needed to find a way to understand it, reconcile it in some way that provided closure.

So I went back to it.

I obsessed for weeks, going through all the public records I could find, learning about the house and about Daniel and his family. I had to know why this happened to me. Unfortunately, aside from the history of the house and the tunnels, there wasn't much to find. Daniel himself was a normal person in the public space, and his family was innocent, so there was no reason to bother them. They had gone through enough. And as for the Bull Man, he turned out to be posing as a janitor from Penn State. There was no official record of him being employed there, but the police found surveillance tapes that showed him on the property. That made sense, given that Jake, Cadence, and me all went there. But still, I couldn't find any connection between Danny and the janitor, and it was killing me not knowing the whole story.

What I did find was information on the house. A man named Thomas H. Gulliver owned Officer Daniel's house during the Civil War, and it was he that discovered this vein in a large flat rock by his cornfield. Actually, he thought it was silver. Lusting after the precious metal, Gulliver enlisted the help of a friend of his who owned an excavation company. These idiots spent weeks digging under this farm and found no silver. However, they did find lead, which fetched a fair price at least. Eventually this vein was mined out, and the land returned to its humble state as a dairy farm.

The farm stayed in the Gulliver family until the nineteen-nineties, when the home went into auction after the late Arthur T. Gulliver passed away. Some family bought the house and sold it to Officer Daniel two years after they got it, and that's when the terror began.

So far as I could tell, the original mine shafts that Gulliver dug crisscrossed under the ground beside the cornfield, which was about a quarter mile from the well. The tunnel I started chained up in, and the main arteries of the maze, the widest tunnels, were all part of the excavation. The tunnel which connected to Daniel's basement, and the narrower tunnels near the well and behind Cadence's chamber, Daniel and the Bull Man had likely made themselves. The rooms ... I found no record of those. No record of the masonry on the walls either, though that could have been standard for that kind of mining. As for the well itself, that was probably there before and had nothing to do with the tunnels originally. I think Daniel connected the excavation site to the well and the house.

All this was easy enough to research, but I wanted to know more. I wanted to know why.

Over time, more information became public, filling in some of those questions of mine. Eventually Danny confessed. Or that was the rumor, anyway. All the media outlets said it a little differently, but either way, the confession wasn't sufficient. When the trial began, Danny pleaded not guilty, and so began the weeks and weeks of prosecution. Ginny kept telling me I shouldn't watch it, but I couldn't help it. I felt like I needed to understand it all more to regain some control of my life.

So much shit came out during that trial. I couldn't believe it. I'm sure there was more too, but these were just the snippets that were presented at the trial. I took it all in with surprising calm.

The Confession Tapes, Part One

The following is a dictation of the police interview with Daniel Jacobson, the Berks County police officer accused of the kidnapping, torture, and murder of more than a dozen people from the Carolina coast to the Greater Philadelphia area.

Officer Chamberlain: "So, Jacobson, my colleagues have informed me that you have requested to meet with me. They said you want to confess. Is this true?"
Jacobson: "That's right."
Chamberlain: "So, it's true, then? You killed those

fourteen people?"

Jacobson: "No, I didn't kill them."

Officer Beck (Chamberlain's partner): "For fuck's sake. I knew it. This is a waste of time."

Chamberlain: "Naomi, please. Officer Jacobson, do you seriously want to do this? You know how this shit works. Don't play games. You either want to confess or you don't."

Jacobson: "I do want to confess, but I want to make sure you understand. I asked for you because you are a man of depth, Chamberlain. If I am going to confess, I want it to be articulated in a way that does justice to what I have done."

Beck: "What? You mean throwing people into a well and chasing them around with a bull head on? Yeah, real articulate, you fucker. You are a disgrace to this department, you know that?"

Jacobson: "Who is the greater disgrace? Me, or the people who worked with me every day and never noticed anything was wrong?"

Beck: "You fucking piece of—"

Chamberlain: "Beck! Please, let me handle this."

Beck: "This is what he wants. Attention. He wants to embarrass us."

Sergeant Kaplin: "Beck, my office, let's go."

Beck: "I hope you fry."

Jacobson: "Good day to you too."

Chamberlain: "Don't think that me entertaining this means I condone anything you have done nor that I am any less disgusted by you."

Jacobson: "Understood, James. All I ask is that you hear my confession."

Chamberlain: "I'm listening."

Jacobson: "Over the course of fifteen years, I have actually kidnapped twenty-two people: the fourteen you attributed to me, plus an additional eight."

Chamberlain: "Twenty-two? Ok; what did you do with the bodies of the other ones?"

Jacobson: "I'll tell you where the bodies are after."

Chamberlain: "So you did kill them? The other eight people?"

Jacobson: "I never killed anyone."

Chamberlain: "But the maze killed them? The bull? Aren't we splitting hairs, Danny?"

Jacobson: "No, we aren't, but I will concede that you may see it that way."

Chamberlain: "But you did kidnap the victims and put them in the maze, correct?"

Jacobson: "Yes. I vetted my victims for weeks, usually. I chose very specific people. It may seem random to you, but it wasn't. There were reasons for each and every person I put in there."

Chamberlain: "Oh yeah? Tell me."

Jacobson: "The audience demanded it. It wasn't my

decision, really. My job was to provide a service, and my service was top notch."

Chamberlain: "You did all this for show? A show for who?"

Jacobson: "I have no idea. Your neighbor, your grocer, your barista, hell, maybe even you. James, people are sick. There is a never-ending demand for the service I provided, and if you think someone else isn't getting ready to stream the next Trial of the Minotaur right now, you're a fool."

Chamberlain: "Trial of The Minotaur? So that's why the bull head? Tell me, how did you come upon this so-called industry for torture porn?"

Jacobson: "Doesn't matter. You wanted my confession, that's the size of it. There are thousands of us, Chamberlain. Good luck shutting them all down."

Chamberlain: "Oh, don't worry Danny, we will. But rewind for second with me. You said you 'carefully selected' your victims. Were those people specifically requested by your audience, or what?"

Jacobson: "My audience did not select the people, but they did select the archetype. You see, they have certain demands, certain pleasures that are to be fulfilled by the Trial of the Minotaur. For example, I chose Lani because of her fighting spirit. Her physical fitness and her mental toughness only added to the pot. The audience loves a fighter because they last longer. It's less boring."

Chamberlain: "So your victims were chosen because they were fighters?"

Jacobson: "Not all of them. The 'protagonist,' if you will, was often of this persuasion, but the others, they could fulfill other desires. Cadence, for example, was for the sadists, the ones who love to see helplessness, who love to watch an innocent, resourceless woman beg for mercy. And Jake, well, he was Lani's counterpoint. His role was to motivate the protagonist and call forth her true strengths."

... There was more to it, trust me, that psycho went on forever, but that was the crux of it ...

Later, during Danny's prosecution, the following exchange occurred (defendant in this dictation is Danny Jacobson):

Prosecutor: "Officer Jacobson, is it true that you kidnapped, tortured, and killed twenty-two people in a maze that you and a Randall Christianson dug out beneath your farm?"
Defendant: "No, that is incorrect."
Prosecutor: "You didn't kill them?"
Defendant: "I didn't kill any of them. The maze killed eight of them, and the Minotaur killed thirteen."
Prosecutor: "Eight plus thirteen is only twenty-one. Are you saying you killed the last victim, or was that also the maze?"

Defendant: "No, the last victim committed suicide. She bit through her tongue after being nailed to a wooden table."

Prosecutor: "You are referring to Abigail Tremont? The woman who you filmed being burned over one hundred times over a three-day period? Burned so much that when police recovered the body over one third of her extremities were stripped of flesh and charred beyond recognition?"

Defendant: "That is correct."

Prosecutor: "So, it's fair to say that you were at least complicit in all twenty-two of these deaths, is it not?"

Defendant: "I only did what my audience demanded. If anything, society is complicit."

... There was more to the exchange, but it was all things I knew, until this section of the trial ...

Prosecutor: "How did you abduct the victims? Were they drugged?"

Defendant: "They were drugged, yes."

Prosecutor: "Did you drug and kidnap each victim, or did Randall?"

Defendant: "Neither."

Prosecutor: "Then you had an accomplice? Who assisted you in kidnapping the victims?"

Defendant: "It was different every time. Always someone dispensable."

Bottom of the Well

Prosecutor: "Can you clarify what you mean by dispensable?"
Defendant: "I think it's rather straightforward."
Prosecutor: "Can you answer my question, Mr. Jacobson?"
Defendant: "I meant I used people who were easy to discredit."
Prosecutor: "Can you provide names? I'll start with Lani Talbot. Who kidnapped her, and how did you interact with this individual?"
Defendant: "I used a student named Jake Thompson to drug her."

... When I heard that I immediately started to cry. I had suspected it when I was in the well, but he ... why had they killed him? It was too much. I had to stop watching that day. Later I went back and read the transcripts, and Danny went on to reveal that the fisherman guy I had seen multiple times was part of it as well. Apparently Jake had drugged both Sami and me, and after the fisherman guy showed up, Danny knew I would call the cops and he would be one of them. When I read this I thought back to that night and realized, it *was* him. I had only seen Danny for a brief moment because he had circled the house to search for the fisherman guy, and his partner, the blonde woman, had stayed with me. I guess Danny offered to sit on the street while his partner went back to the station.

After Sami and I fell asleep he came in and got me.

My best guess as far as when Jake got me must have been when we were swimming. I had set our drinks beside the pool. He could have easily slipped something in, and if he did it toward the later end of the evening, well, it would have only been thirty to forty minutes before Sami and I ended up alone in my apartment. It could take an hour or more for the drugs to really take effect, depending on the dose. Danny never said what kind of drug it was, but I could only guess that was the timeline.

As for Sami, he was never abducted. He woke up the next morning on the floor in my living room, confused and in a daze. When he realized what had happened, Sami immediately notified the authorities, as well as Ginny and my dad, and a search had been started. That explained why the police responded so quickly to Ginny's claims that I was held captive "on some farm somewhere outside of town." I spoke to Sami a few times following my rescue, but our relationship never went anywhere. When he saw me after I was released from the hospital, he told me he was sorry for letting everything happen to me, for not protecting me, and I strongly refuted him; nothing was his fault. We tried to have coffee together a couple times, but I just didn't have the capacity for it. After that, we never spoke again, except the occasional "hello" in passing.

The final piece of the puzzle was that the Bull Man

apparently waited in Jake's backseat and drugged him using Chloroform when he was getting into his car after leaving Cole's house. They had threatened Jake somehow to convince him to drug me, but then they killed him anyway to avoid loose ends. That was how they did it every time, with all the previous victims, Danny explained.

After the transcripts, there were records of the evidence presented by the prosecution. Among them were the feeds from Danny's dark web experience. Apparently, the FBI was able to retrieve the feed from Danny's phone even though the server had long been deleted, because he kept the footage as sort of "trophies."

The first thing they found in Danny's hidden files made me sick. Every time I thought humans couldn't be more repugnant, more came to light ...

Evidence Logs #7

Type: Encrypted files from Defendant, Daniel Jacobson's phone

Description: Decrypted files found on the defendant, Officer Daniel Jacobson's cellphone, were recovered from being previously deleted. The files were found to be connected to a ring of smut streamers on the dark web hereafter referred to as the "Minotaur Ring." The following "Admin's Guide" was recovered, in addition to several chat feeds (to follow).

"Admin's Guide"

The first fifty entries into this virtual codex are populated by absurd, seemingly random images of historical/mythological places, creatures, or tools. Sometimes the images are accompanied by text, sometimes the images stand alone. Every few pages, the user is prompted to answer questions. Officer Jacobson explained this is how the Trial of The Minotaur Experience Leaders are confirmed, though even when pressed Officer Jacobson was vague as to how these images and questions correlated to being chosen. Once chosen, the experience leader, or "admin," was given this document:

Bottom of the Well

"Fear is pain arising from the anticipation of evil."

~ Aristotle

5 points of emotional interest ...

1: Anxiety

2: Test of Will

3: Fight or Flight

4: True Test

5: Climax

Be aware ... outcomes may pale to perceptions

Be Vigilant. Be Patient. Be Objective.

These are the five stages of fear. To create the most intense, intimate experience, you must achieve them through natural progression. You may be tempted to explore your authority as your audience implores you to, but react not hastily, for it is your duty as the administrator of this trial to provide a true test of the human spirit for both the watchers and the participants.

Death is the consequence for failure to uphold the doctrines of the Trial of the Minotaur Experience.

This is your trial now. Use these simple tips and make it your own:

Anxiety: You must embed the fear before it becomes a reality. Evoke Aristotle's quote. Darkness, suppression of free will, unfamiliar sounds/smells/textures, and especially uncertainty are all ways to create anxiety

Test of will: This is not a single event. You must chip away at the protagonist with choices, false hope, and psychological torment.

Fight or Flight: Make them decide to live or die. Do your worst.

True Test: Unveil your game, make them prove it to you.

Bottom of the Well

Remember, the game has to winnable.

Climax: Either the protagonist dies or wins and escapes. You must not interfere with this outcome. If the protagonist wins, you will be protected. This is done to ensure the integrity of the trial.

Good luck. Enjoy this honor bestowed upon you as you host The Trial of the Minotaur Experience.

There are really no words to describe the realization that there were entire communities out there thinking this stuff up. And then, there were these streams. This shit was the most disturbing of all ...

Evidence logs #17

Type: Video Feed from Defendant, Daniel Jacobson's cellphone

Description: Retrieved deleted feed from a dark web server that was traced back to the defendant's IP address. This feed depicted victims Lani Talbot, Cadence Smith, and Jake Thompson being subjected to physical and psychological torture inside of a maze hidden below the defendant's farm. Participants in this video feed paid the defendant for the right to watch as these events occurred. None of the participants were identified but some have been found to have participated in previous video feeds depicting other victims in the maze. This feed is one of many we believe are all connected to the same ring of smut film peddlers on the dark web. This particular series has been dubbed "Trial of the Minotaur" by the participants. Although victims are also subjected to physical violence in these "trials," the specific focus of this ring seems to be psychological terror. No connections have been made to other ringleaders at this time, but it is hypothesized that Daniel was one of many who contributed content to this ring.

The Feed:

Excerpt 1:

Admin: Welcome back. And thank you all for your patronage. You are going to love this run.
#1: good to be back. Who we got?
#2: This is the Minotaur's Trial?
#3: Hello all!
#1: @#2, ...
#4: Only 2 people?
Admin: Yes, this is the Minotaur's Trial, and no #4, there is another. This is a continuation of a previous feed.
#2: WTF?
#5: The blonde one is still in here?
#1: You came here right #2? You a cop?
#5: nvm I see her now
#3: Yeah blondie still on the spikes
#5: saw her yeah. Boring AF
#4: Oh, it's a continuation. Blonde girl isn't dead? Who's the Latina? She hot
#2: not a cop, fuck you #1
#1: fuck me? I'll fucking kill you

Admin: Keep it about the Trial or you will be banned. Only people I have invited have access. There are no cops. And to those who were not on the last feed, Cadence, the blonde, has been in the maze now for 54 hours. Lani (the Brazilian girl) and Jake are just waking up after 2 hours in the maze. I'm changing the camera feed occasionally so we can see Cadence. We only did this one other time, where we added people in mid-run, but it got great reception and some of you asked us to do it again, so here we are. I hope you enjoy this surprise.

#5: Awesome! You guys rock!

#6: Just joined, looks like fun. 3 people? I love it!

#5: right? Could get really messy

#1: Are you going to make them kill each other?

#5: that'd be awesome

#4: That's stupid. Make 'em think they can rescue each other. That's better

#7: don't care either way, just make 'em bleed

#2: @ #1, you know I can trace you IP? You in Albuquerque.

#1: lol come get me kid

#3: Wow. @ #4 Y she smokin

#4: right? Srsly can't wait to hear her scream

#5: break her, cut her, drain her

Admin: She WILL be broken, in due time. Be patient.

#1: She's so stupid. Look at her feeling the wall like she can really get out

Bottom of the Well

#7: nice try bitch

#4: is there audio?

Admin: Now there is.

#4: ok good

#5: They always say the same shit

#6: right, like it makes a difference

#4: She's so hot. Can't wait until she starts screaming

#7: Can we make requests on this feed?

Admin: Yes. We will consider all requests, though not all will be fulfilled. Every Trial of the Minotaur is a test of psychological will. It is not meant to be solely murder for smut. Please keep the objective of the trial in mind when beseeching the Minotaur.

#5: Look at her! She's trying to pull the chains out of block LOL

#7: Ok, good. I don't want them dying quickly. You should make her break her wrist to get out

#1: Yeah @ #5, typical reaction. Logic doesn't matter. The dude is doing the same thing

#6: Make the dude break her wrist haha

#4: rape her. Put her face in the dirt and put rocks in her mouth

#3: YES

#7: Ok but don't rush it.

#1: The Minotaur doesn't usually do rape

#4: usually?

#2: Yo, when's he coming anyway? Minotaur?

#1: STFU #2

Admin: Patience. In due time.

Excerpt 2:

#1: Is it time?

#4: Oh yeah, she look broke as fuck

#6: The guy still in the maze?

#7: yeah, just showed him a min ago

Admin: The feed is up for the next hour. Time to vote: how do you want the Minotaur to punish Lani if she takes the key?

#7: Break her fingers so she can't use it lol

#3: Nah, let her escape but cut off a toe on each foot. Watch her try to walk out

#4: you know my opinion; shove her in the dirt. Destroy her soul

#2: Skin her arm. Then throw salt on it and bandage it up so she doesn't bleed out

#1: no you have to give her a goal and keep her thinking there is hope. I like the toe, but only one foot so she can still limp along. The point of the challenge is it has to be POSSIBLE

#7: Stake her to the ground

#6: what?

#1: Crucifixion?

#7: Yeah. Face down, so she can't move. Make her pull the spikes out if she want to live

Bottom of the Well

#2: I love it

#6: How's she gonna get out if she can't move?

#5: She'll figure it out if she wants to live

#1: Make sure the spikes are long enough to hold, but narrow enough that her hands aren't useless after

#7: YES and leave the key where she can see it to motivate her so she keeps trying like a good little girl

#4: She's gonna wail like hell when Minotaur pounds those into her flesh. I LOVE this. Although, I would like to see her skinned alive. Maybe later.

Admin: Staking it is. The Minotaur is gathering materials now. Stay tuned.

Excerpt #3:

#5: what's happening, just joined

#1: They found the well

#5: Any action yet?

#1: Nah

#7: They showed the blonde. Minotaur made some fresh cuts

#5: Aww, I missed it?

#2: It was ok. Wish he would either kill her or let her off the rack. It's boring AF

#3: Can't kill her yet. She Lani's motivation

#2: true

#1: Nice touch giving him the flashlight

#7: Yeah, you see her body language? She thinks he is in on it

#1: Right. That's why we gave him the key, right? To fuck with her.

#4: Hey anyone ever actually climb out the well?

#1: I've never seen it.

Admin: We wouldn't allow it. The perception of escape is part of the game, but if anyone wants to escape the Minotaur's Trial, they have to find the real exit.

#2: You all think she will escape?

#3: Meh

#1: no

#4: Well, aren't we gonna vote on how to kill her? Is she even allowed to escape?

Admin: If the participants solve the puzzle, they are allowed to escape. Otherwise, it wouldn't be a trial.

#4: .....

#7: No one ever escapes though no worries

#4: I paid good money to see this. I want her dead

#6: I agree

#5: I guess she can escape, but I want her to suffer more first

#1: she will

#4: NO I WANT HER FUCKING DEAD CHOPPED TO PIECES THROWN IN A GARBAGE BUCKET AND SPIT ON!

#2: Relax bro

#4: I WANT MY $$$$ BACK IF SHE WALKS AWAY

Bottom of the Well

Admin: You all agreed upon entering the Minotaur's Trial experience that you were paying for the chance to observe a true test of will to endure psychological and physical torture. It was disclosed up front that this is not a pay-for-murder room, nor was it ever stated that certain outcomes were guaranteed. Part of what makes the Minotaur's Trial so seductive is the idea that participants can theoretically escape. If they could not escape, there would be no hope to crush, and it is that feeling of breaking a person's spirit that we are all seeking, is it not? As a final note, I want to remind all of you on this feed that I know who each of you are, and if you are unhappy with the content or the way this series is conducted, I suggest you do not come back in the future and leave it at that. You may not like my answer if you want to press the issue.

Excerpt 4:

#2: wow, ok, they found the room

#1: doesn't matter not the exit

#3: How u know?

#6: Seen ppl get here b4, no exit

#7: yo, she got the shoes. Gotta raise the stakes b4 she get cocky

#2: They have too much. Time to break morale

#4: Break bones, break morale.

Admin: Time for a vote: How to punish them for entering

the chamber of the Minotaur?

#2: Even the odds. Kill one

#1: agreed. Kill Jake

#6: Kill Jake, take Lani's flashlight. Chase her in the dark again.

#4: Cripple Lani, chase Jake away leaving her behind. Use the mallet, smash the shit of her ankles and break her kneecaps

#5: No fun. I like watching her run

#1: kill Jake and make her watch. Then make her run

#2: Kick that kid into the spike pit

#4: why make her run? You want her to be scared? Break her fucking legs and lock her in that room.

#7: @ #4, hell yeah, game over Chica

#4: that's right. You're dead bitch. All you can do is lay there and cry and bleed to death. DO IT! Minotaur! I'm begging you for Brazilian tears!

Admin: It is decided. Please stand by.

... There were a few more excerpts, but honestly, I couldn't stomach it anymore. The fact that such fucked up, evil shit existed out there, beyond the shield of our sheltered everyday existence ... I just wish I could unknow it.

The trial finally ended, and Danny was sentenced to the death penalty, the first death sentence in Pennsylvania since 1999. If anyone deserved it, it was sure as hell Daniel Jacobson. I remember when the judge dropped that gavel, when the sentence was declared loudly and with great resolve. The camera panned to a corner of the courthouse, where Daniel's wife sat watching, her face stained with tears. As the camera found her, she had begun a fresh spout of tears, her face flushing instantly as she leaned over the row of seats in front of her. They weren't tears of sadness, at least not for Danny. I thought she was crying in the same way that I cried when I learned about Jake. From confusion, disbelief, and betrayal. She was sad because she had been lied to and used for years, and the judge's gavel just confirmed it. Her and her two daughters has witnessed someone they loved and trusted for years unfold into the greatest evil a person could know, and now ... they were broken. I wanted to reach through my phone and hug her. None of this was her fault.

After that day, nothing happened for a long time. There were appeals, but all were denied. The FBI never found any co-conspirators of the Trial of the Minotaur experience, to my knowledge. I still get scared thinking about the possibility that those people are out there, that there was probably another maze somewhere and that at any given moment, more people were being tortured. But I had to stop thinking about it.

I did my best to move on. It took a very long time and honestly, even at my best, I'll never be the same. There will probably always be a fear of certain things inside of me, like being in the dark or feeling confined or restrained. To cope with that, I kept going to therapy, and at the advice of my counselor, kept myself busy. After everything settled down, I just couldn't focus on sports medicine. I still loved track and lacrosse, and I still played, but I had to do something else. So, I changed my major. Criminal law felt more productive. At the time, I had no specific plans for retribution or anything, but it did cross my mind, the idea of finding the rest of those sick fucks running the Trial of the Minotaur. I had some ideas about where I'd start looking, but I wasn't sure if I had the will. Still, it felt right to get a law degree because even if I never pursued the dark web ring, I'd still get a chance to make a difference to people, to bring justice to those who were savaged by the worst of humankind. Plus, it kept me busy. Kept my mind off things.

In my junior year, I met a woman, Amy. I had been reluctant to let anyone in for so long, but four years after the Trial of the Minotaur, I was finally feeling ok enough to take the risk. And she was so sweet and so understanding. Even when I couldn't always give her all of myself, she was patient with me. She'd had some trauma of her own, but that's a whole other story. The part that mattered was that she understood me and she was there for me. I married her the year after graduation and we bought a house together outside of Philadelphia, where I took a job at a big law firm.

Life after that was ... quiet. I'd say I was happy. As happy as a person could be after going through what I went through. I still hadn't decided if I wanted to pursue the Bull Man, to subject myself to the experience again. I wasn't sure I could. But I'd devote my life to justice all the same, and no matter how things turned out, I promised myself I'd never give in. I'd never settle for letting the fear control me. I was stronger than that now. I was a brave, wise, intuitive, and resilient woman with plenty of love still left in my heart to overcome anything.

I was a survivor.

And I'd never forget it.

Patrick Carpenter

A word from Author Patrick Carpenter

I was born and raised in New England, and now live in Maine with my family, working as a banker by day and a husband, father, and writer all other times. From humble beginnings writing and telling fantasy stories to friends on the playground in grade school to writing my first full length novel, Dark Ocean, in 2020, I've always been engaged in the craft of storytelling. My top inspirations are the works of Steven King and Orson Scott Card, with such titles as Ender's Game (Orson Scott Card) and The Girl Who Loved Tom Gordon (Steven King) being among my favorites. I write and enjoys reading most genres, but my true passion is found in sci-fi/fantasy, with a particular affinity for mixtures of magic and futuristic, sometimes dystopian worlds. My flagship series, Dark Ocean, has been described as "Avatar the Last Airbender meets Star Wars," and that's very accurate!

Bottom of the Well is my first attempt at the horror genre, and I had a great time finding inspiration and trying to craft a truly suspenseful, horrifying work. So much so that I intend to write more horror very soon! I hope you'll follow me at **epicartspc.com** and check out my future work.

Explore more from Author Patrick Carpenter:

Dark Ocean:

In a galaxy far from and long since the existence of Earth, Addy Palmer and her brother, Alex, struggle to live amongst the corruption and post-war chaos of the Sarian empire. Every day seems like just another pessimistic drop in the bucket for Addy. Then, one day, everything changes when Alex inadvertently discovers that he has a super-human power. This phenomenal event is witnessed by a man named Zach Brine, an obsessive and meticulous soldier from a secretive organization called "Prism," binding them together on an epic quest to discover the origin of Alex's power.

Along the way, Addy seeks to discover meaning in her life that was once defined by hopelessness and nihilism. Wondrous worlds, mystical creatures, and kindred spirits open her heart to all that is possible. Unfortunately, her journey also reveals a long repressed, tormented past involving a warlord known only as "The Fox." Now awakened, Addy cannot take back what she knows. Can she overcome it and find her true purpose? Will she be able to help Alex find his? Most importantly, can she do it without losing herself in the process?

Coming soon ... Dark Ocean: Soul of Fire

Nearly two years have passed since Lynn Palmer defeated the Grothian warlord known as "The Fox," and the unifying effects of Lynn's conquest have brought the Sarian Empire closer to permanent peace than ever. But nothing last forever ...

Captain Zach Brine and the rest of the crew of Leviathan are sent to the neutral world of Corinth to oversee a peace summit, but an insidious new political faction composed of both old grudges and new ambitions rises up and launches an attack on the Corithian capital of Zalia. With both sides blaming each other, progress is quickly falling apart. But Lynn realizes there's a much greater problem ... the leader of the rebel faction is no ordinary Corithian. Could he be like Lynn and Alex? If so, how did he obtain his power?

When faced with the answers, Lynn Palmer must choose: Mercy or Annihilation. There can be no other way. The shards are her destiny. The only thing she doesn't know ... what will it cost the people she loves?

Planned Horror Release for 2023 ... Eyes

Four biology students at the University of Maine venture into the Saco Bay to collect samples for a routine lab project when they encounter a mysterious island that has never been there before. Upon investigation, the students find the island is populated by species of plants and insects never identified before. Plus, there's this strange energy ... almost as if the island itself is watching them.

The next day, the island is gone, as if were never there, and strange emotions begin creeping into the brains of the students. Almost as if someone is controlling them, feeding their minds with insidious plots.

It's ok.
Manifest it.
Feed the Wolf.

Bathe in their blood.

Made in the USA
Coppell, TX
21 December 2022